CROCODILE CREEK: 24-HOUR RESCUE

**A cutting-edge medical centre
at the heart of a community.
Fully equipped for saving lives and loves!**

**Crocodile Creek's state-of-the-art Medical
Centre and Rescue Response Unit is home to a
team of expertly trained medical professionals.
These dedicated men and women face the
challenges of life, love and medicine every day!**

An abandoned baby!
The tension is mounting as a new-born baby
is found in the Outback whilst a young girl
fights for her life.

Two feuding families!
A long-held rivalry is threatening the well-being
of the community. Only hospital head
Charles Wetherby holds the key to this bitter battle.

A race to save lives!
Crocodile Creek's highly skilled medical rescue
team must compete with the fierce heat of the
Australian Outback and the scorching power
of their own emotions.

**PREGNANT WITH HIS CHILD
is the third of four continuing stories from
Marion Lennox, Alison Roberts, Lilian Darcy
and Meredith Webber. Join them at Crocodile
Creek every month until June in
Mills & Boon® Medical Romance™**

Dear Reader

Sometimes writers are asked to do a series of linked stories with a group of other writers, using a basic idea created by our editors which we then expand. I've had great experiences with these twice in the past, both times getting to write a story I never would have thought up on my own. One had a strong fantasy element involving mermaids, and the other was set in the world of professional yacht racing, so I got to relive my childhood *Little Mermaid* dreams as well as vicariously strapping myself to the rail of a maxi yacht in a storm while the waves threw me around like a rollercoaster. This latter experience was definitely better in the imagination than it would have been in real life!

With our **CROCODILE CREEK: 24-HOUR RESCUE** series, however, we four writers came up with the idea of working together ourselves, and we generated the basic storylines as a group before taking each individual book away and writing it on our own. We had several cosy and excitable sessions in a hotel suite during a writers' conference, brainstorming characters and ideas—I can neither confirm nor deny that chocolate and champagne were involved in the planning process—and here is Book Three in our four-book series.

If you like our fictional town and its characters, please let us know, because we would love to have a good reason to return, in our imaginations, to Crocodile Creek.

Lilian Darcy

If you enjoyed this story,
look out for Lilian Darcy's next book
THE MILLIONAIRE'S CINDERELLA WIFE,
available July 2006 in Tender Romance™

AMD

00426207

F

md

PREGNANT
WITH HIS CHILD

BY
LILIAN DARCY

MILLS & BOON®

First published in Great Britain 2006
Harlequin Mills & Boon Limited,
Eton House, 18-24 Paradise Road, Richmond, Surrey TW9 1SR

© Lilian Darcy 2006

ISBN 0 263 19083 8

Set in Times Roman 10½ on 12½ pt.
15-0306-50798

Printed and bound in Great Britain
by Antony Rowe Ltd, Chippenham, Wiltshire

CHAPTER ONE

DR CHRISTINA FARRELLY had only one significant item left on her 'to do' list for today. She hadn't written it down. It wasn't something she was likely to overlook.

Dump Joe.

Driving to the airport to pick him up in the sweet, warm darkness of a typical North Queensland autumn night, she felt sick about it.

Heartsick.

Sick to her stomach.

She didn't want to do this.

And even this early in the piece it wasn't working out according to plan, anyhow.

His flight from Cairns had been delayed and he was getting in six hours late, which meant that the almost bearable scenario of having a private late-afternoon coffee at her place while they talked about it had morphed into the utterly non-bearable scenario of delivering him direct to the doctors' residence at eleven o'clock on a Sunday night, gabbling at him, 'Dumping you, sorry, but fixed you up a room here,' and laying rubber all the way down the hospital driveway as she screeched her car off into the night.

No.

She really could not do *Dump Joe* that way.

Not when she didn't want to end their relationship at all.

Maybe the flight delay was an acceptable reason to put it off.

The airport was only a few kilometres from her house, an old-fashioned Queenslander a couple of streets back from the commercial heart of Crocodile Creek, which she'd inherited from her grandmother several years ago. The big creek itself flowed in a slow, lazy curve between the town and the airport, while a smaller tributary curved with equal laziness between the airport and the hospital before joining forces with Crocodile Creek just a hundred metres before it spilled into the ocean.

The main road crossed Crocodile Creek's wide streambed over a bridge that was slated to be replaced very soon. Construction on the new one, a hundred metres upstream, had recently begun. Christina would be sad to see the old bridge go, but, then, maybe she had a tendency to hold onto things...hopes...relationships...for longer than she should.

Dump Joe.

Yes, no excuses, no delaying tactics, just do it.

To get to the modest-sized passenger terminal, she had to skirt around the emergency services headquarters and the runway for fixed-wing aircraft, with its rows of night-time guidance lights staring at her balefully the entire way.

The whole place was close to deserted at this hour. Joe's flight would have been the last one in tonight. She saw it still taxiing towards the terminal, bringing Joe ever closer to an emotional crisis—or merely an incomprehensible, irritating disappointment?—that he had no inkling of as yet.

Other people did have an inkling. Mike Poulos had guessed that something was wrong last week when he and Christina had flown together in the Remote Rescue chopper to bring in a heart-attack patient from an isolated location, but he wouldn't have said much to anyone else, both because he was a decent, non-gossipy kind of guy and because—well—he had much better things to think about right now.

He and Emily Morgan, after knowing each other for a good eighteen months without a ripple to ruffle the surface, had suddenly discovered they were madly, ocean-churningly in love, *marriage-mindedly* in love.

And, oh, lord, she shouldn't think about it in such a bitchy way, she liked both of them a lot, but…how come everyone else could connect the dots and come up with the obvious answer when Joe Barrett wouldn't even admit to the existence of dots in the first place?

Turning into the car park, Christina felt the tears starting and blinked them back. Shoot, if she was crying about this now, before she'd even done it, said it—how bad was the actual conversation going to be?

And how bad was it going to be when the news had travelled all around the hospital?

Or had it done so already?

In a foolish attempt to distance herself from the reality of what she was doing, she'd involved Brian Simmons in his role as hospital administrator, asking him to organise the room for Joe at the doctors' residence. This was the original bush nursing hospital, over a hundred years old, and it was situated on the grounds of the current, much more modern set of hospital buildings that provided the nexus for Crocodile Creek's outback air medical service.

Most of the single doctors lived there, but Christina never had, since she had her grandmother's house, with its lush jungle of garden screening the cool privacy of a wraparound veranda, its antique-filled rooms, its peace and tranquillity. And because she had a spare room in that house, and because Joe was only in Crocodile Creek for one week in four, he'd become her part-time boarder two years ago.

He hadn't stayed in that limited role for very long.

The doctors' residence was a noisy, welcoming and very pleasant place, and Christina dropped in there quite often. She liked most of the medical staff currently living there, but she didn't want them asking questions behind her back, worrying about her, telling each other that they didn't understand what was going on because Christina and Joe had always seemed so *good* together.

They would do and say all of that, of course.

There was only one factor that might dilute it a little. The past couple of weeks at Crocodile Creek had been pretty dramatic ones, starting with Simon-the-cardiologist and Kirsty-the-intern sneaking off into the sunset together, followed by the far more serious discovery of a critically ill newborn left for dead after an outback rodeo, and a head-on collision in the outlying settlement of Wygera which had left four young aboriginal kids dead and others still hospitalised down south.

'People do have other things to think about, Christina Farrelly,' she scolded herself, punctuating the statement with a wrenching pull on the handbrake of the car.

The newborn was doing well now. He had a mother, Megan Cooper, who'd almost died herself following serious post-partum complications on top of the traumatic belief that her baby had been born dead. Over the past few days, Megan had slowly begun to recover. And he had a name.

Jackson.

He didn't yet have a known father—Megan wasn't saying anything on that subject—or grandparents who'd been told of his existence. Meanwhile, the community at Wygera would take months to find its feet again…

Yes, everyone in Crocodile Creek most definitely had other things to think about.

But right now all Christina could think about was that mental 'to do' list, and the item right at the top of it.

Dump Joe.

When she reached the arrivals area of the almost-empty terminal, passengers were just starting to come through the gate. There were no fancy jetways at this airport. Joe would be walking across the open tarmac with the other tired arrivals, while the luggage-cart swung in an arc around them through the humid press of diesel fumes, beating them to the baggage claim area by a scant minute.

With the flight only half-full, Christina had no trouble spotting him. He stood half a head above the tallest of the other passengers, and he was broader and stronger, with darker skin, a wider smile… He had always seemed to her to have so much more than anyone else she'd ever met.

More heart.

More energy.

More strategies for keeping their part-time relationship in exactly the place he wanted it.

Which had slowly and inexorably become a place she just couldn't bear for it to stay.

Dump Joe.

'Hi,' she said, her voice wobbly.

'Tink.' He buried his face in her neck, inhaling the scent of her hair in open appreciation. 'Oh, Tink!' He was the only person who ever called her Tink. Tunk, really, with his strong New Zealand accent. 'Hell, I've missed you.

Mmm, you smell so good!' And he was the only person who ever made her feel this way when he hugged her.

Tingling.

Exultant.

Weak with need.

Where she belonged.

And, tonight, utterly miserable.

She felt his mouth press hard against her hair, her cheekbone, the corners of her lips. Hungry kisses, but they promised nothing.

'I am wiped!' he said. 'Seven hours in the transit lounge in Cairns.'

'Do you have a bag?'

'Nope. Everything's here.' He patted the heavily packed overnight bag that swung on his shoulder. Beneath the white band of his T-shirt sleeve, the smooth skin of his upper arm bulged with muscle, and the thin, braided shape of his blue-black tattoo was visible. It looked like a bracelet, and made a clearer statement about his part-Maori ancestry than did the honey colour of his skin. 'Let's go. Are you on flight duty tomorrow?'

'Yes, I'm due back here at seven, for a clinic run.' On the opposite side of the runway, really, but it counted as the same place.

'And I'm rostered on from eight. Still, we can grab a bit of time tonight, eh?' His dark eyes flicked down at her, with that familiar sense of a shared secret in their depths, and the total confidence that she wanted exactly what he did. Her body stirred and her heart fell.

'Yes, we need some time.' The words were neutral. Far too neutral. He should have noticed. Or was he simply too tired to hear them as significant?

Dump Joe.

She really, really had not wanted to have to do it like this. For his sake, or for her. They would have to talk at her place. She wasn't going to say everything here in the airport car park, or with the car engine idling outside the doctors' residence.

As they drove past the hospital, he commented, 'Quite a few lights on there tonight, in the house and in the main building.'

'We've had a busy couple of weeks.' She filled in some of the details. The personal as well as the medical.

There was Cal's engagement to Dr Gina Lopez, the American cardiologist he'd known in Townsville five years ago, and who'd turned out to have given birth to his son, CJ, now four years old. There were Kirsty and Simon, Emily and Mike, the car accident at the Wygera settlement, and darling, heroic baby Jackson and his mother.

'He has von Willebrand's disease, on top of everything else, brave little sweetheart,' she finished. The rare blood disorder had been diagnosed after Dr Lopez had been alerted by the unusual amount of bleeding from the baby's cord stump. It was treatable and shouldn't cause ongoing problems now that they knew about it.

'So the mother has it, too?' Joe asked.

'No, she doesn't, and neither do the mother's parents— although her dad's health is pretty iffy in other areas, apparently—which means the carrier must be the father. But so far Megan isn't telling us who or where he is. Dr Wetherby's father had von Willebrand's, apparently, but if there's a family connection he knows about, he's not saying. It could be a coincidence.'

'Whew!'

'That pretty much sums it up.'

She hated having so much news to dump...*dump*...on

him all in one big, stodgy mass. It always happened, even when events in Crocodile Creek weren't nearly as fast-moving as they'd been this time around. Joe spent three weeks out of four at home in New Zealand.

Or possibly, for all she knew, on the far side of a worm-hole leading to a distant galaxy.

No, OK, that was a slight exaggeration.

Over the two years they'd been a part-time couple, he had let slip a few salient facts. He lived in Auckland. He'd done his medical degree at Auckland University. He worked in a group general practice. He wasn't married. (But he could be lying. Was he lying? Would she know?) He had a mother, a younger half-sister, a stepdad.

But he made it painfully clear how much he hated talking about his life at home. He never phoned her from New Zealand. He'd given her both his home and work numbers there 'for an emergency' but the handful of times she'd eagerly dialled those, early on in their relationship, he'd again made it clear that the calls weren't wanted.

He didn't do it nastily. Christina wasn't convinced he had a nasty bone in his body.

He did it with an upbeat, warm-voiced energy. 'Listen, Tink, I can't talk, OK?' Didn't suggest a better time. Didn't phone her back. Didn't mention the phone calls the next time she saw him.

She'd begun to feel that she was the equivalent of a sailor's girl in every port. True, Joe kept coming back to the same port, and it was apparently a port he really, really enjoyed, but that didn't change the basic fact about their relationship. Christina's life was an open book to him. She'd told him an-ecdotes about her childhood, dreams she had for the future, beliefs about what mattered in life. But in return she was his 'rest and recreation', his R&R, as the American navy seamen who occasionally berthed to the south in Townsville phrased it, and that was very plainly all he wanted from her.

Which did suggest that he might be married.

No! No…

She'd never caught him out in a lie, and didn't want to launch into a paranoid confrontation. It wasn't her style.

And it almost didn't matter if he *was* married. The point was, for whatever reason—and the fact that she had no real idea of the reason was a problem in itself—this relationship was going nowhere, while her biological clock had hitched a ride on a racehorse some time last year and was contemplating the imminent switch to a faster mode of transportation.

Christina was thirty-three. She had a sensible head on her shoulders. She wanted marriage and a family with a decent, honourable man. She didn't want to stay perpetually at the 'young, in love and having fun' stage with a man she only saw for a handful of hours each month, no matter how nice that was while it was happening. Joe knew that. She hadn't said it straight out, or put on any pressure on him, but he had to know it from the way she talked about her brother's kids in Brisbane, her admiration for her parents' marriage.

If there had been any sign of a deepening in Joe's commitment, if he'd started sharing more of his life in New Zealand with her, if she knew why he kept the boundaries so firmly in place, she would have been prepared to wait a lot longer, but there was none of that. He was a couple of years younger than her, but that was no excuse.

She was also the faithful type, and if she was ever going to find a man who wanted what she wanted, she was going to have to get Joe Barrett well and truly out of her system before she started looking.

Which didn't give her the luxury of putting things off and had thus led her to where she was right now, at eleven o'clock on a Sunday evening, approaching the past-its-use-by-date bridge over Crocodile Creek with a gorgeous man beside her in the car.

A man who was also past his use-by date.

A man she was about to dump.

Even though she really, really didn't want to do it.

There was a grey humped shape lying in the road, just a metre before the bridge.

'Kangaroo,' Joe said, sitting up higher in the passenger seat. He craned to look at it as Christina slowed the car. 'Was that there ten minutes ago when you came across?'

'I don't think so.' She skirted it and the tarred planks of the two-lane bridge went thunkety-thunkety-thunk as she drove across. 'No,' she added, more certain about it now. 'No, it wasn't.' Because she'd been thinking about the bridge, about not wanting to see it go. She'd have noticed.

'It's dangerous, anyhow. We should stop and get it off the road.'

She slowed further and looked for a place to turn, which was easy to find at this time of night when there was so little traffic. The kangaroo had been unlucky, in the wrong place at the wrong time. Back on the far side of the bridge, she parked safely on the shoulder and walked across to the still, silent shape in Joe's wake.

'Yep, it's still warm,' he said. He felt its neck. 'But it's dead, all right, poor thing.'

Except that just then it moved.

No, not the mother, Christina realised, the joey in her pouch.

'Crikey!' Joe said. 'There's a little fella in there!'

'Don't start doing your crocodile hunter imitation, Joe Barrett!'

She couldn't help laughing. For a man who'd just spent around eleven hours in transit, on top of a solid week of general practice, he'd summoned up his energy and his good humour pretty fast. He was always like this. Loved the chance to get a laugh out of a situation. Never complained for long, just got on with things.

The way she had to do, as soon as they got home...

'I could do my British wildlife documentary presenter instead,' he offered.

She summoned another smile. 'No, because you're terrible at him, too. Just be nice and male and masterful for me and tell me what we're going to do.'

Because I'm tired and stressed and I wanted an excuse to put off the dumping-you conversation, but not this kind of an excuse.

'Well, we can't leave it, Tink.' He was working as he spoke, carefully dragging the warm, soft body of the mother safely off the road and turning her so that they could gain access to the pouch.

'I know that. I wouldn't want to.' She gathered herself, focused on the right priorities. 'There's the park, up towards the mountains—would that be best? They have a sanctuary and an animal nursery enclosure. We'd have to wake up the ranger.'

'He'll handle it.' From the size of the movement they'd seen, this joey should be big enough to survive the loss of its mother, as long as it hadn't been injured itself.

A ute rumbled across the bridge with a load of bulging garbage bags bouncing in the open tray at the back. It slowed.

'You right there, mate?'

Christina recognised Bill Doyle, owner of the Black Cockatoo Hotel.

'Dead mother, living joey,' Christina summarised quickly. 'Hi, Bill. It's me, Christina Farrelly.'

'Oh, hello, Doc. You're branching out into the vet business now?'

'Something like that. We thought we'd take it up to Atherton National Park, to the ranger.'

'Right you are, then.' He nodded, and drove off, happy to leave them to it. He was obviously heading to the town rubbish tip.

Christina and Joe shared the task of examining the joey, which was half-grown and should have been thrashing its gangly, growing legs around in terror, but wasn't. Huddled in the pouch, it had its eyes open and it was breathing fast, but there was no obvious sign of injury.

'We do need to get it to the ranger,' Christina said. 'We can't feed it or take care of it ourselves.'

'I'll grab my sweatshirt from the car,' Joe said. 'We'll wrap it in that.'

It was awkward and both of them narrowly escaped getting scratched by the sharp toenails at the end of those long legs, but once Joe had the animal on his lap in the car, all bundled up tight, it seemed to settle again.

Christina got behind the wheel and drove.

The highway leading to the south-west was dark and empty, apart from one lone long-haul truck that roared past at one point, making her wonder about the driver's schedule and the chemical means he might use to keep himself going. On a couple of the main highways down south, cameras captured licence plate details at certain points on the route and truckers were fined for making the journey in too short a time, but out here that wasn't practical. The accident rate was higher than it should have been.

'How's he doing?' she asked Joe.

'He's good. Quiet. Breathing.'

She risked a glance across.

Joe and a joey, both good, quiet and breathing.

Her stomach sank as she thought again about rocking the boat.

The truck slowed. Was it stopping for him? It had to be. Yes! Yes!

The big rig ground to a laborious halt and he ran after it, eager to seize on the first piece of good luck he'd had all day. Make that all year. His whole life, it felt like.

This was an omen.

'Looking for a ride somewhere, mate?' the driver said.

'Yes.' Anywhere. 'Over the ranges.'

'Hop in, then.'

It felt so good. To be off his feet. To be moving. He'd been standing there for hours and no one had even thought about picking him up. Did he look that much like a deadbeat or a criminal?

Evidently.

Other people had thought so. Her father, for example. Her.

His love.

The reason for this journey.

His mates would laugh if they knew he thought this way about her. Like some soppy male lead in a soppy film who can get any girl he wants but can't forget The One.

Not that you can get any girl you want, you drop-kick. How many do you even meet?

But he didn't care. He was the soppiest of the lot. He just wanted her.

He'd been turfed off her parents' property in a blast of anger so intense it had driven him five hundred kilometres north, and he'd really believed the old man might kill him if he went back.

But the loss of her from his life had taken the heart out of him. He should have fought harder for her, he should have stood up to her father's anger. Why had it taken him so long to get it right? Why had he let other people make his decisions for him?

He couldn't understand the person he'd been back then. He'd toughened up since, a lot, because it had been months ago, and you'd never know now that he'd grown up pampered in Sydney—private school, bloody violin lessons, of course you can learn to ride if you want, darling, which had meant tutoring in dressage, not the bush horsemanship that he knew was in his blood.

So if the drought-crazed old man killed him, or tried to, so be it. He'd fight back a lot harder than he could have done six months ago. He'd had his twenty-second birthday last week. He'd shaken off a lifetime of parental mollycoddling. He could show her, now, how much his love was worth and maybe she'd leave with him this time, leave her father and her mum, and it'd all be OK.

Yes, sitting here high in the cabin of the big rig he could see it, how it would all work out, as long as he could get to her, see her and talk to her and be with her even just for a few precious hours, show her what he was made of, before he had to turn around again and head back north tomorrow, noon at the latest, or lose his job and the three months of precious back pay that was owing to him.

His boss hadn't wanted to let him go at all, but he'd managed to squeeze just these few days before the big cattle drive began. They were moving the beasts hundreds of kilometres between properties, starting next week, and taking a route through rough country that stirred something deep in his spirit. If he could hear from her own mouth that she still loved him, he'd go droving with the feeling that he owned the whole world.

'As far as the turn-off to Mount Evelyn. Is that far enough for you?' he heard.

'Sorry?'

'I said I'm only going as far as the turn-off to Mount Evelyn.'

'Right. OK.' His heart dropped like a spent firework.

Talk about omens!

This guy was going a tenth of the distance he needed. Less. He'd never get there before morning. His stomach rumbled. He should have stopped for a hamburger and chips in Crocodile Creek, but he hadn't wanted to lose the precious time. That seemed stupid now. He wasn't going to get to her tonight. He'd have to go back, leave it for weeks more. He hadn't thought this through.

Talk about omens.

This one, he'd listen to.

He couldn't see that he had a choice.

It was almost midnight by the time Joe and Christina reached the park entrance. The boom gate was closed and locked, but a four-wheel-drive such as the light one she drove could skirt around it if she moved a couple of half-rotted logs.

Joe had reached the same conclusion. 'If you take Junior here…'

'No, I'll do it. He's quiet, don't disturb him.' She jumped out while she was still speaking, and the job was easy in her sensible jeans, T-shirt and running shoes. The T-shirt wasn't quite adequate warmth-wise. They'd climbed around six hundred metres from the coastal plain, and at this hour on a May night, it was chilly.

'You're an Amazon,' Joe teased her when she got back in the car.

I'm going to have to be, she thought. And she wasn't thinking physically.

They knocked at the front door of the ranger's house five minutes later, and roused his wife. 'Don't worry, I was up with the baby anyway. Oh, look at him, he's a gorgeous little fella, isn't he? Yes, we can take care of him, he's big enough, and we have a couple of others so he won't be lonely.'

She offered a cup of tea, and her sleepy husband appeared, but Joe and Christina looked at each other and wordlessly reached the same conclusion—which happened quite often. They didn't want to keep these two up in the middle of the night, or themselves out, driving on an inadequate rural road, any later than necessary.

'We should get back,' Joe said. 'Shouldn't we, Tink? We're both working full days tomorrow.'

This time he drove, which gave Christina too much time to think.

I can't do it tonight. But I won't sleep if I don't. Oh, I won't sleep anyhow. It'll be impossible in the morning, we'll both be scrambling to get out the door and get to the hospital and the base. I can't leave it, though, not if I'm really going to say it. That room is waiting for him, and people will be wondering what on earth is going on. Maybe now, while we're driving?

She got ready. Tried to. Took a deep breath and prepared herself to say his name. *Joe, we have to talk.* But then she let the moment pass. She was a coward!

They came to a bend and he veered around it, seeming not fully in control. His breath hissed out sharply between his teeth. 'That's not right,' he said.

'What, Joe?' She touched his shoulder instinctively, her open hand dwarfed by its warm bulk.

'Think we've got a flat tyre.' He slowed the vehicle carefully and pulled onto the verge.

She erupted into silent, stress-filled laughter. 'You are joking! Just tell me you're joking, Joe Barrett!'

'Uh, no. That's just slightly the last straw, isn't it?' Joe said.

'You got that right!' More than you know, Joe.

If she believed in omens, she would have taken good notice of this one, and decided that somebody up there really didn't want her to dump Joe tonight. But she didn't believe in omens—didn't believe her personal life warranted quite that much cosmic attention—so she just gritted her teeth and thought, Maybe while we're changing the tyre?

Which was indeed impressively flat. It was the front left one, while the bend Joe had taken curved to the right. No wonder he had struggled to keep control of the vehicle.

As they'd done when they'd examined the joey, they worked together in silent harmony. Joe set the hazard lights flashing. Christina got out the jack. Joe positioned it and wound it up till it was in the right position to take the vehicle's weight. Joe stomped his foot on the wrench to loosen the nuts while Christina detached the spare from its big bracket on the rear door.

He was so strong! She felt a crippling wave of longing

wash over her as she looked at him, and it was hard to drag her eyes away. *I won't be able to look at him this way after tonight. I won't have the right to. And it'll hurt too much.*

Together, they took off the damaged wheel and manoeuvred the spare into position, then took turns tightening the nuts.

Joe grinned at her when they were done. 'Love a woman with axle grease on her nose,' he said. 'Ver-r-ah sexy.'

'Joe, we have to—'

Talk.

Too late. He kissed her, a raunchy, confident, full-bodied, sweet-tasting smooch on the mouth, anchored in place with his hand, which was no doubt leaving more grease on her jaw… Oh, and probably a smudgy handprint on her backside as well. When he pulled away, he was still grinning, and he was so gorgeous, big and full of life and gorgeous. She couldn't utter any fateful words to him right now.

She couldn't have uttered them anyhow. They weren't alone.

'Hey!'

'What the heck—?'

'Hey, wait! Wait!' A figure came jogging towards them, out of breath and frantic for their attention.

Joe waved and nodded, then muttered, 'Not our night, is it?' He put the jack away and closed the back door of the four-wheel-drive. He and Christina both stood waiting and watching as the figure approached. It was a man, a young man, not nearly as big and tall as Joe but well built and strong all the same.

He came to a halt, panting, and Joe asked sharply, 'What's wrong?'

Christina knew he'd be thinking about an accident, some kind of emergency. It happened out here. As doctors, they'd seen more than their share of the unexpected, and there weren't many ordinary, innocuous reasons why someone would be running along a deserted highway like this one in the middle of the night.

Not many ordinary reasons, but this was one of them. 'Can I hitch a ride?' He looked as if he wasn't that long out of his teens. Twenty-one or twenty-two.

'Into town? Home? You from around here?' Joe asked.

'No, but, yeah, I'm heading into town.' He didn't offer an explanation as to what he'd do when he got there, and the admission that he wasn't local had been hurried and edgy.

Christina and Joe looked at each other again. They really had to take him. He didn't look dangerous. But what was he doing here?

'Hop in the back,' Joe said, then added casually to Christina, 'You OK to drive again?'

She nodded, understanding the direction of his thoughts as she so often did. If this guy did turn out to be trouble, it made sense for big, strong Joe to be the one with his hands free.

'What's your name?' Joe asked, as Christina sped up along the road.

'Uh, Jack.'

Joe and a joey. Wheel jack to prop up the car, strange Jack appearing in the night, hopefully not planning to carjack Christina's four-wheel-drive. It was too far past her bedtime for any of this.

'You look like you were a bit stranded back there,' Joe said. 'We had an errand up at the park headquarters, but we didn't pass you on the way up, did we?'

'Think I passed you,' Jack said. 'In a truck. But the driver turned off to Mount Evelyn. He reckoned someone else might still come through, but I got cold and no one did, and—yeah.'

'So you turned round?'

'Yeah, and you passed me—I was off to the side—and then I saw your hazard lights flashing through the trees, and so I ran.'

'Where were you headed?'

'Ah…just one of the stations out west. To see a friend. I'm on a station further up. I'm a stockman, and I had a couple of days off. Thought I could make it, but I just didn't get the rides.'

For someone who'd been reticent, not to say cagey, at the start, after five minutes they couldn't shut him up. He discoursed on the pitfalls of hitching, the need for rain. It must have been the relief at getting picked up when he'd resigned himself to a cold, lonely night of walking back towards the coast.

He wouldn't have let Christina get a word in edge-ways, even if she had been happy to dump Joe in front of a total stranger. He seemed quite bright, articulate. And there was something about the way he talked, a sugges-tion that he was deliberately lowering the pitch of his voice by a couple of notes, roughening the edges of his accent.

If he was working as a jackeroo, that made sense. City lads with cowboy fantasies could get given a rough time up here if they didn't fight back. This one looked strong enough and intelligent enough to make his way—although not, perhaps, when he was hitching.

'Should have known I couldn't do it in two days.' He sounded defeated suddenly, as the lights of the base and the town came into view. 'My…my mate would probably have been…' He paused again. 'Yeah, busy anyhow.'

They reached the T-junction a couple of hundred metres south of the hospital and air rescue base, where the highway to the west joined the coast road. 'Where should we drop you?' Joe asked their passenger.

'Oh. Here? Right here is fine.' The reticence was back in place.

'You've got somewhere to go?'

'Yep. No worries.'

'If you're sure,' Joe said. 'Because we can take you into town.'

'Nope. It's fine.'

OK, he'd had his chance. If he was sleeping rough, it wouldn't matter. Down here at sea level, the temperature was several degrees warmer, and there was no rain forecast. They let him off at the junction, and Christina glanced at him a couple of times in the rear-view mirror. He hadn't moved by the time the dip of the road towards Crocodile Creek took him out of sight.

'Was he real?' she asked Joe.

Or had he been sent by a meddling cosmos to prevent her from biting the bullet on the big break-up talk?

All her tired, repetitive thoughts came crashing back into place. *I don't want to do this. I'll leave it until tomorrow. But we're both working all day. If someone at the hospital—bloody Brian—mentions the room at the house…*

They crossed the bridge and reached the overhead lights in the main street. Joe looked at his watch. 'Sheesh, it's a quarter past one!'

'I'm wide awake, though.'

'Yeah, me, too. Buzzing. And filthy. Remind me, Tink.' He grinned across at her, and her heart did its ninety-seventh lurch of the evening. 'Where were we, before we were so rudely interrupted?'

On the edge of a precipice, Joe. That's where we were. But she didn't say it.

CHAPTER TWO

THEY GOT OUT of the car and went inside. Joe put his overnight bag down in the middle of the living-room rug and hugged her again. Blissfully. His arms were hard and warm and familiar, he made a hungry, appreciative *mmm* sound deep in his chest, he rubbed his strong, smooth jaw against her cheek like a cat.

Christina felt the familiar stirring of desire. It began low in her stomach and radiated outwards like the heat from a glowing coal, and it hadn't lessened or lost its dizzying sense of importance in two years. In fact, it had only grown stronger. Because she had always been so unsure of how long Joe Barrett would stay in her life?

He kissed her.

And, oh, she shouldn't let him do this, but if it was for the last time…

At some level, had she wondered if every kiss would be their last?

She couldn't hold the question long enough to really consider it. It was too abstract. All she could think about was now, because there was no 'maybe the last' about this kiss. This time she knew for certain.

His mouth teased her, clinging and tasting, lavishing her

generously with hot sensation. He was never a man who did things by halves. (Except that this didn't gel, did it? Their relationship was only a half, or even less. A lopped-off, uncompleted thing.) He was never a man who did things by halves *in the present moment,* she revised fuzzily. He kissed her with his whole soul, his hard-packed male energy, his astonishing heart, and she kissed him back.

For the last time.

She ran her hands up the back of his head, releasing the scent of his shampoo into the air. She drank in the taste and feel of his warm mouth and pushed deeper, wanting more, wanting to get still closer, never wanting this to end. Time was standing still right now, but it couldn't stand still for much longer.

Joe was the one who broke the moment. 'I need a shower,' he muttered, still holding her. 'Smell like a plane. And probably kangaroo. I'm amazed you're letting me do this.'

So was she.

She was appalled that she was letting him do this, appalled that she couldn't even smell plane or kangaroo, she could only smell him.

'I need a shower just as much,' she said out loud.

'Wanna share?' That teasing sideways grin came at her, that sexy, dark-eyed look from beneath deliberately lowered lashes. He rubbed his jaw against her cheek and her head turned all on its own, her mouth once more in search of his.

Christina Farrelly, you have to be stronger than this, she coached herself.

'No, you go ahead and have it to yourself,' she told him. So hard to say it. Even harder to let him go. 'I—I'll just wash up in the laundry sink. I don't have the Cairns transit lounge to wash off.'

'I'd still like to share,' he said. He pulled her back against his chest, teasing her, so confident about how she'd respond. He had no idea.

'Joe, we have to talk,' she blurted out. Her heart started to pound as soon as the words were spoken.

Crunch time.

Moment of truth.

'Yeah?'

His big dark eyes were puzzled but untroubled. He still didn't see it coming. Why should he? She hadn't given any hints or warnings. She hadn't known until a week or two ago that she'd reached ultimatum time.

Make this easier. Make it civilised.

If that was possible.

'Are you hungry or anything?' she offered vaguely, waving her hand in the direction of the kitchen. Then she caught sight of the clock. Almost one-thirty. If she was really going to do this tonight, it was way past time.

She was going to do it. She'd said that first fateful line about talking. She had to go through with it now. Bringing her hand to his shoulder she felt another sudden, sick-making lurch in her guts.

'Hungry? No,' he said. 'We got a fistful of meal and drink vouchers in Cairns to make up for the delay.' He studied her face more closely, his own softening. He bumped his nose lightly against hers. 'Hey, what's up? Something else has happened? You didn't tell me everything in the car? What were you waiting for?'

His tone had dropped to the intimate pitch that she loved. It was the voice he used in bed, the voice he'd used last month when a gastric upset picked up from a patient had laid her low for the last two days of his visit. 'Still feeling crook, Tink?' he'd said several times.

He'd had to fly home while she'd still been spending a miserable amount of time in the bathroom and maybe that was when she'd begun to understand once and for all that she needed more—more than a man she only saw once a month, in the snatches of time where their long working hours didn't clash.

Should she tell him to sit down? She was the one with the shaky knees, because she didn't know where to start. 'This isn't going anywhere, is it?' she blurted out. 'Us, I mean.'

'Going anywhere?'

'Joe, don't be thick about it.' Shaky knees and a shaky voice. 'Don't make it harder. Please. Take a second to think about it and then try and tell me you don't know what I mean.'

She tore herself from his touch and began to pace around the room, wishing it was bigger, wishing he'd trap her and pull her back into his arms. She felt claustrophobic, and desperate for him to pre-empt this and tell her she didn't have to say it.

So far, he wasn't doing so. He'd stilled, retreated to lean his broad shoulder against the open archway that led between this room and the dining area. He looked as if he wanted to touch her and hold her again but had decided that he shouldn't.

'I want you to move out,' she said. 'Tomorrow, if you can. I can't bear to drag this out, and I can't imagine you'd want that either. I've arranged a room for you at the house.'

There was only one house, the doctors' residence at the hospital. It should be spelt with a capital H.

'I can't keep going with this,' she went on. 'We've been together—a quarter together—for two years. More. And I want…more. More, Joe. Some idea of a direction. Commitment. Some indication that…that this isn't just time out for you. You know, the Christina Farrelly full-service day spa. I—I—' *Oh, hell, I'm going to say the L word.* '—love you. You have to know that by now, surely, and what we have just isn't good enough any more.'

Silence.

Around three seconds' worth.

'I love you, too,' he said slowly. 'Is that what this is about? That I haven't said it? I love you, Tink.'

But he was floundering, and the way he said it told her that the other shoe was about to drop.

He swore. Which was unusual. Especially with such force.

'I'm sorry you're not happy.' He took a breath. 'I'm a bit, um, stunned that you're not happy. It's one-thirty in the morning. We've had a hell of a night. And you're suddenly saying all this.'

'You thought this was what I wanted? All I wanted? For it to go on like this forever? It's not sudden, Joe.'

'We have such a great time together.'

'You think that's all I want? A great time?'

'Better than a miserable time.'

'Don't joke about this. Don't.'

'I'm not belittling—I care about you. I love you. I'm— yeah—stunned.'

She closed her eyes, then opened them again. He'd said the L word, too. Three times. But it was just a word. Some men could splash it around like wet paint. *Yeah, 'course I love ya, babe.* She hadn't picked Joe as being one of them. 'Sorry, I'm being a bit slow here, Joe.' Her voice came out slow and rusty. 'Are you fighting this?'

Please, please, fight it!

'No. I wouldn't. Fight it. How could I? If that's what you're saying you want. If you've…' He swore again, and for the first time he sounded angry. '…arranged a room.'

It's not what I want! It's not!

'I've got no grounds to fight it on,' he said. 'If it's how you feel. But, hell, Christina, you couldn't have given me a bit more of a warning? Told me at the airport, or—?'

'I didn't think we'd get sidetracked on the way home.'

'You could have phoned me in Auckland.'

'You hate me phoning. You *never* phone me.'

He didn't deny it. He was too angry. 'You've arranged a room!'

'That was the best thing to do, wasn't it? Make it easier, on both of us?'

'Guess you can look at it that way.'

'But…' OK, time to lose all pride here, and give him a hint.

Oh, this was miserable! She hadn't realised quite how much she'd been hoping the room at the doctors' house would stand empty after all, throughout her process of decision-making, when she'd arranged the room with Brian Simmons, all through the sad and farcical delays in their arrival home tonight.

'You mean you're not going to promise anything different in the future?' she asked.

He whooshed out a sigh, then groped for the right words. 'I don't feel as if I've promised the wrong things so far. I mean, I'm only here one week in four. You said it yourself. I really like being with you, Tink.' His tone lost some of its angry edge. 'I think we're good together. Great together. My life at home—I know I never talk about that. To be honest, I think the main reason I come here is not the extra money, even though, heaven knows, I need that, but the fact that I don't have to think about home…' He stopped. 'It's tough. My life at home is tough. It's so good to have you, and not to talk about it, or think about it—'

'This is your R&R, isn't it? Your time out?'

He seized on both expressions, grateful for them. 'Yes! And it's so good!'

'Not for me, Joe.' She could hardly get out the words. Sobs wanted to come out instead.

'No?' he said softly.

'The word "love" obviously means something very different to you. Not what it means if I say it. I want to be part of your life. Your whole life.'

This time his answer came quick as a rabbit trap clamping shut. 'No, you don't.'

'So you're not going to tell me anything about—'

'No. I'm not.'

OK, two choices.

One, accuse him of having a wife.

Two, storm out and slam the door.

Christina did neither. She just started shaking so hard that Joe couldn't have missed it from a distance of three hundred metres. Couldn't have ignored it unless he didn't care anything for her at all.

And he did care.

He came up to her, wrapped his arms around her, physically held her on her feet so she wouldn't subside onto the rug with her face buried in her hands.

'I am so sorry, Tink,' he whispered. 'I didn't see it coming. Maybe I should have. That crack about warning me, and the room—that probably wasn't fair. I can see how you feel. Couldn't we just try and…?' He stopped.

'Yes?'

He didn't say anything, just kept holding her. Oh, hell, and she so loved the way he smelled, even tonight when it came tinged with the faint aromas of aeroplane, axle grease and kangaroo. She didn't know what it was. Him, his soap, his clothes. He always smelled like this and she always loved it. Could have drowned in it. Could have saved her life with it.

'No,' he finally answered. 'I'm not going to argue. I've got no grounds. Nothing to promise. Nothing to offer. Hurts, it's stupid. I'm stupid. Sorry. I've been an idiot not to realise that you'd want things spelled out more clearly. I'm not in the market for something long term, for a commitment. I'm just not. I have enough of those. I just don't have room and, really, you wouldn't want me to.'

'But you won't let me be the judge of that,' she said, in a voice that managed to be hard and wobbly at the same time. 'You've just made the decision for me, without telling me—'

'Can we stop this now? Can we? I think we have to, because I don't think there's any point in saying more, or anything more we can say.' He pulled back and stood very upright, chest like a board, arms folded over it. She could see what he was doing, mentally clawing his way back to a less emotional operating mode, getting some distance.

She tried to do the same.

He was right. They'd reached the impasse she'd…only one-quarter expected, to be honest. Less than a quarter. Ten per cent. She only now fully realised that she had seriously been hoping he'd throw his arms around her and tell her it was all a mistake, he wanted everything that she wanted, and that he'd make all the right promises on the spot.

But, no, they'd reached an impasse, and there was nothing left to say.

'Are they…uh…they're not still expecting me at the house tonight?' he asked. 'At this hour?'

'If your flight had been on time, that was the plan. But now we should wait until tomorrow. I was thinking so even before the joey and the flat tyre. No one's had enough sleep over there the past week or so. I don't want to go thumping around those loud wooden floors and turning on lights at two in the morning.'

'My stuff…' Which had accumulated to several suit-cases' and boxes' worth over the past two years.

'I'll be out on the clinic run till almost dark tomorrow. Where are they slotting you at the hospital?'

'Don't know yet.' Joe was always used where he was needed. The emergency department, Maternity, Paeds, An-aesthesia occasionally.

'If you can drop me at the base, you can have the car,' she told him. 'Then if you get a break during the day you can pack and shift. I didn't…box anything up for you be-cause…' She didn't finish.

'That's OK. Hell, that's OK, Tink. I wouldn't have ex-pected for a second…' He didn't finish either.

'Have your shower. I'm going to bed,' she gasped, and didn't wait.

Not for an answer, not for a protest.

She knew nothing would come.

And, of course, she couldn't sleep.

At two-thirty she stopped listening for the sounds of him moving around the house. He'd obviously gone to bed, too. At three she stopped thinking about going along to his room and climbing into his bed…or hoping that he would come along and climb into hers. At three-thirty she surren-dered the idea of phoning the obstetrics and gynaecology unit at the hospital in the hope that Georgie Turner or Grace O'Riordan would be there, delivering a baby.

If they were, they wouldn't have time to talk. If they did have time, Joe would hear her sobbing on the phone. And sobbing and talking wouldn't even put a dent in the pain.

At four she got up to get a glass of water in the kitchen and came back to meet Joe padding silently along the passage towards her, wearing only his black cotton pyjama pants and an inadequate cloak of darkness over his bare chest. They did one of those silent movie–type byplays where two people both moved in the same direction to try and get past each other and almost collided three times, accompanied by fervent apologies. But it wasn't funny.

'Are you married, Joe?' she said.

'No!' His protest tailed away to a rough whisper. 'Hell, no, I'm not married!'

'Well, that's something.' It sounded very bitter.

'Ah, Tink, ah, hell. Don't do this.'

'Do what?'

'Don't look for reasons.'

'Aren't there reasons?'

'Of course there are.'

'Then tell me what they are.'

But he didn't answer, because they were already holding onto each other like shipwreck survivors in a dark sea. His whole body was warm from sleep—or maybe from frustrated wakefulness—and she could feel the low ride of his drawstring waistband against her lower stomach through the thin stretch cotton of her sleeveless pyjama top.

It was so familiar. The way her breasts pressed against him. The rapid burgeoning of his arousal. The tickle of hair, the rumbling groan of need he made, the rippling sensitivity of every square inch of her skin.

Christina didn't mean to let it go as far as it did, but when he started kissing her, seeking her mouth a little clumsily in the darkness, she just didn't care about self-preservation or pride or boundaries. He felt so good, and she wanted him too much, the way she always had.

He didn't ask out loud how far he could go, but his body asked the question with every deepening kiss and every more intimate touch, and he never got no for an answer. The door to his room was only a few feet away, so that was where they ended up, sitting on his bed.

She could just see the faint swimming of light in his dark eyes, the sober expression on his face.

'Christina…' he breathed.

He peeled her top over her head and bent to kiss her breasts and her neck. She closed her eyes, letting him, just letting him do it, then she reached out and spread her fingers in his thick hair, pulled his head up and kissed him so hard they were both grateful for breath at the end of it.

He stood, pulled her up, slid her pyjama pants down then his, taking his own nakedness and state of arousal for granted. She'd seen it before. She'd responded to it in a hundred wonderful ways. This time it would be as good and as powerful as ever. Still standing, he touched her, gliding his hands lightly over her body, all the expected places and some unexpected ones as well. The backs of her knees, the knobs of her spine.

He was taking inventory, storing up memories, as aware as she was that this was the last time. It really was. It had to be. No secret hopes in her heart this time. 'Christina…' he breathed again. His hands grew slower and lighter on her skin, hardly touching her breasts, whispering down her body.

Suddenly she felt angry and impatient and didn't want to wait, didn't want to linger over this as if it was some great elemental parting, made unavoidable by war or destiny. This was his choice, and it didn't have to happen. She had set the challenge, but he had failed to rise to it, so how the hell could he act as if they were playing out some twenty-first-century version of *Romeo and Juliet?*

Let's just do it, Joe, slake our needs and move on, if that's all you've ever wanted from me.

She grabbed his hips and rolled them both onto the bed so that he was on top of her, his weight threatening to flatten her breasts and challenge her lungs. Then she wrapped her legs around him and guided him into her with rough haste, lifting her body to meet his first instinctive thrust.

'Hey…' he growled.

She didn't answer, just held him tighter with her legs, lifted herself harder against him, straining to feel that exquisite sensation of total fullness. Then she began to rock, knowing what it would do to his control, wanting to punish him and give to him and prove how wrong he was, all at the same time.

He swore, and groaned.

Then he gave in.

No turning back now.

Sensations dovetailed and began to spin like water diving into the hollow centre of a whirlpool. Christina closed her eyes. She didn't need sight. She had all the information she needed about Joe's state of mind from other sources—the whip-like motions of his body, the sounds wrenched from deep inside him, the grip of his hands.

And then she stopped caring even about those things, stopped knowing where his body began and hers ended. They clawed their way higher and higher towards release, and it was wonderful, long and hard and intensely satisfying, but seconds after it had finished, her spirits had plunged again and she wondered what on earth she'd just done.

Made everything even harder?

Given him a send-off he'd never forget?

Lost even the illusion of having taken the assertive approach?

They lay together for a few minutes, breathless and still, but she couldn't bear it and eased her body out from beneath his arm, needing the bleak safety of her own bed. 'Stay,' he growled, clamping a hand to her hip.

'I can't, Joe.'

'OK. OK.' His hand went slack and he let her go.

For the second time that night, he wasn't going to fight for her.

CHAPTER THREE

MORNING CAME way too quickly.

Christina heard evidence that Joe was already up as soon as she'd turned off her alarm. She hid in bed for several minutes, but couldn't postpone the inevitable, so she scrambled into the bathroom and succeeded in keeping clear of him until a five-minute overlap in the kitchen, when she managed to down a glass of juice. The idea of anything more substantial made her feel ill, and yet her empty stomach scarcely felt better.

'So I'm dropping you at the base?' he said.

'Yes. We can go now, if you want.'

'OK. Then I'll have time to look at the room.'

They were tense with each other this morning. The care for each other's state of mind had gone, and of course so had the comfortable teamwork between them that had been so apparent last night when they'd dealt with the joey, the flat tyre and the hitchhiker.

The emotional nakedness had gone, too—the willingness to say, *I love you.*

Joe was angry that this wasn't fun any more, that Christina had rocked the boat and changed the rules. She was angry that fun was all he wanted, that he would go to such lengths to stay inside his comfort zone, even when she'd shown him so clearly that she wanted more. That hurt so much that it had to be someone's fault.

And it's not mine, Christina thought. She felt totally drained.

She looks as wiped as I feel, Joe decided as he drove.

When he'd taken her phone number off a hospital staff notice-board two years ago and had called her about the boarder she was looking for—'reasonable rent, shift worker OK, own room, share bathroom'—he hadn't thought about the possibility of something like this.

He'd started out at the doctors' house, but had known pretty fast that it wasn't what he wanted. He didn't need the potential for clashing personalities, compulsory partying when he wasn't in the mood, minimal privacy. He was there to work, to make money and get a bit of breathing space. Christina Farrelly's place fitted the bill perfectly.

Roughly fifteen minutes after first setting eyes on it, and on her, he'd known that he wanted both the room and the woman. She was just the kind he always went for. Attractive in a natural kind of way, with a supple figure, some nice curves, bright brown eyes that knew how to laugh and dance, dark hair in a swinging ponytail and a smile that was more urchin grin than Mona Lisa mystique. She had a healthy energy, a bright mind and a depth of kindness that you couldn't fake.

She didn't play games.

He didn't either, so it hadn't taken him long to get across to her how he felt and what he wanted. It had been easy, not planned. One morning they'd been in the kitchen together, making silly little apologies to each other every twenty seconds as they'd crossed paths, preparing their separate breakfasts. She'd been standing by the toaster, waiting for it to pop up, with her hand leaning on the benchtop, and he'd just come up to her and laid his own hand on top.

She hadn't taken hers away—he hadn't seriously feared that she would—and it was all the communication either of them had needed. Their arms had gone around each other, their lips had met, they'd pressed their bodies together, they'd whispered a few things.

Oh, that feels so good. You knew I wanted this, didn't you? I think your toast is burning.

Two years later…

He might have been way too slow over the past couple of months to pick up on the fact that she wasn't happy with the state of their relationship anymore, but the blue shadows beneath her brown eyes and the tight muscles in her face this morning were concrete details impossible to overlook.

Her body language said a lot, too—the way she was hugging up against the passenger door, her legs angled away from him and her shoulder in a tight, protective curve.

Yeah, he felt angry about it.

Angry with her, angry with himself.

And anger was what he dealt with at home so much of the time. It was exactly what he loved about coming here, about the time he spent with Christina—that he could relax and laugh and get out and have fun, revel in that whole side of himself, bring it out in her, and just not have to feel angry and responsible and overwhelmed.

Well, the illusory sense that Crocodile Creek was a different, safer, happier, easier and more benign universe had been stripped away now. When he glanced across at her, he didn't see safety and peace any more, he saw only a whole new set of problems. He wanted to grab her by the shoulders and yell, *Why did you have to rock the boat, when it was all so good?*

But it wouldn't be fair.

When they reached the Remote Rescue base, nurse Grace O'Riordan was just zipping into a parking place out front in her battered little car. Tink made a little sound and sat up straighter when she saw her. A spark of relief, Joe realised. She and Grace were friends. They'd talk.

In fact, everyone would talk. It was that kind of hospital, that kind of town.

His heart sank. He got enough of this at home, especially when he was out anywhere with Amber. It was an anonymous kind of attention then, way less personal than this, but still it brought the same neck-crawling awareness that you were being talked about behind your back. Amber was fantastic, the way she dealt with it. Joe was the one with issues.

He said tightly to Tink now, 'We can talk about keys and things later in the week, can't we?' He'd be flying home on Sunday. It seemed like a long time away, and he had no idea if the time would drag or rocket by.

She nodded in reply, tried to smile, gave up on the attempt and just climbed out of the car. He watched her walk over to Grace, then wheeled the car around and sped towards the hospital, his whole being in rebellion against the way everything had changed.

The doctors' house was a hive of early morning activity. Cal was still in residence with his rediscovered love, Dr Gina Lopez, and their little boy, CJ, although they were looking for a place together in town. Hamish McGregor was mooching around, complaining about the weather, which was a bit rich coming from a Scotsman. His contract would be coming to an end very soon, and he'd be going home. Charles Wetherby, the hospital's almost legendary medical administrator, had a few staffing problems on his hands at the moment.

'So you shouldn't all be bloody looking at me,' Joe muttered under his breath as he opened the noisy back veranda screen door and stepped into the kitchen.

He fielded the chorus of greetings, managed a couple of jokey, blokey lines, ignored the undercurrents and asked, 'Which room's for me, does anyone know?'

Emily Morgan hopped up from the table. 'I'll show you, Joe.'

Chatting about plumbing quirks and shopping rosters, she led him along to a cool, dark space that opened onto the side veranda about halfway along. Those French doors in each room were what saved this place, he considered. You could actually come and go through them without the whole world being aware of the fact. Provided you learned where the creaking boards were, he revised, stepping onto the veranda and hearing an agonised groan from the wood beneath one foot.

'No one minds if you put a chair or two out here,' Emily said. 'It's peaceful when no one else is around.'

'Does that ever happen?'

She laughed. 'It's been known. There's even a degree of tact involved, occasionally.'

Hamish appeared out of the next door along at that moment, wearing scrubs and in a hurry. 'Lucky,' he flung back at both of them.

Emily made an anxious sound and watched him go.

'It's OK,' Joe said. 'I can do without tact. You're right, I don't feel particularly lucky right now. I thought Christina was happy to—Yeah. Anyhow.' He stopped suddenly as he saw the stricken, embarrassed look in Emily's grey-blue eyes.

'Oh,' she said. 'Joe. Gosh. He was talking about the baby. Not you and—I'm sorry, did Christina fill you in?'

'Fill me in?' he echoed.

Fill me in? Oh, by the way, Joe, I'm ending our relationship and you're moving into the doctors' house. *Of course she filled me in!*

'That's why I'm here, isn't it?' he said bleakly. 'Looking at the room.'

This whole thing was awkward enough, without him and Emily talking at cross-purposes. Who was being slow here?

Me, probably, he thought. My head's a mess.

'Th-the baby from the rodeo,' Emily said, stammering with remorse. She was quite shy at times. 'We didn't have a name for him at first, so we called him Lucky and it stuck, even though he's officially Jackson Cooper now. And I'm just a bit worried, seeing Hamish go haring off like that.'

'It's unexpected?'

'Yes, and we all have so much invested in the little guy now. Megan and the baby have both been doing so well, adjusting to each other nicely. They'll be discharged once we can sort out the family situation a little better, and the feeding. At the moment, her parents don't even know she has him, and she's refusing to go back home. She's only nineteen. If something's gone wrong…'

'Right.' That was all he could say. 'That wouldn't be good.'

Emily touched his arm. 'Listen, about you and Christina. I'm sorry I misunderstood. People are going to talk, of course, and *not* be tactful, but it's only because we care about both of you. It's none of our business, I know.'

'That's OK. It was my fault.'

She nodded, looked as if she was about to say something more, then decided against it. 'I'll let you settle in. You're working today, aren't you?'

'Should get across there in a couple of minutes,' he told

her, so that she would go away. They both knew he didn't have to be in that much of a hurry.

When she left, he took a proper look at the room.

Ah, hell, this was so typical!

Christina had made up the bed. He recognised sheets she sometimes used at home. She'd stacked some books on the bookshelf. He knew she must be the one who had done it and that these weren't simply the discards of a previous resident, because he recognised the names of authors he liked. No one else here in Crocodile Creek knew him that well.

No one else knew what brand of toothpaste he used, and that he was finicky about not getting a thick, dried-up collar of minty green stuff around the top of the tube. No one else knew the music he listened to on a lazy Sunday morning. No one else knew the silly voice he put on when he talked to friendly cats.

Because it was *rubbish* what Christina had said about her not being a part of his life! Even if he never talked about home, they knew each other. And what they had together was important, even if it was part time and focused purely on the present. How could she accuse him of not being a part of her life?

She'd even put flowers on the bedside table to relieve the slightly spartan atmosphere—some bright, trailing things that came from her own garden. He knew that because she always made the effort to have flowers around her own house, too.

His heart twisted and he hated himself because of how much he'd hurt her, because of the way this had hit him out of the blue, and because he still didn't believe that he had it in him to offer her more. It wouldn't be fair on either of them.

* * *

It was impossible to talk in the plane. Without earphones, the noise level was too high, and with them…well, who wanted to bare their soul into a plastic headset? On the ground during their pre-flight routine, Grace had given her a pat on the shoulder and a sympathetic smile, which had told Christina that word had begun to spread about her break-up with Joe.

And my face must be a front-page headline all on its own, she realised.

They only had two clinic stops today. The first one would be the shortest, at a cattle station to the north-west owned by a huge pastoral company. At around eleven-thirty, they'd make the hop from there to Gunyamurra, the tiny town not far from the rodeo ground where baby Jackson Cooper had been found eleven days ago.

'It was like one of those earthquake miracles, Christina, don't you think?' Grace said into the headphones as they flew. 'You know, when newborns are found alive after days buried under rubble?'

'I guess it was,' she answered, obedient to the need to respond to Grace's happiness about it. Grace was a great nurse.

The clinic at Amity Downs was uneventful, a textbook extract on the kinds of problems they encountered in these isolated regions. Stress-related illnesses exacerbated by the drought, minor injuries that hadn't been taken care of so that they'd become infected, routine check-ups, including prenatal care for women who faced the prospect of a long journey to hospital when their babies were due.

Arriving at Gunyamurra, they set up some equipment in the tiny Country Women's Association hall that doubled as a clinic during the visit they made here every second week. The air in the building was rather musty. The CWA ran a mini lending library, and as well as a handful of current paperbacks there was a larger selection of old Australian classics—Mary Grant Bruce's 'Billabong' series, and lots of Ethel Turner. They were lovely books, but rarely borrowed these days and probably filled with mould spores. As usual, Christina opened all the windows.

Then it was time for a break for lunch before the first patients were due. Since the dusty town didn't run to a café or sandwich shop, everyone had brought their own.

'And I've got a flask of hot water for tea,' Grace confided to Christina.

She betrayed her Irish heritage in her fondness for it—strong and milky and sweet. The same heritage was clear from her freckled skin, blue eyes and amazing laugh. You had to be in a pretty bad way if you didn't find Grace O'Riordan's laugh contagious. It burst beyond the confines of her slightly too plump torso and cascaded like a musical scale, and Grace could find a reason to laugh at almost anything.

'Let's not sit in this stuffy clinic building, drinking the urn water out of mugs that predate the invention of radio,' she said.

'And probably haven't had a proper wash since.'

'Exactly. We can find a tree to sit under. And I thought, you know, you might—'

'Yes, Grace, I do want to talk!'

'That's the spirit.' Grace's eyes were twinkling and sympathetic at the same time. 'Bring it all up, like a dodgy meat pie.'

Christina laughed. The sound ended on a half-sob. 'Oh, bloody hell, Grace, this just feels so bad! I knew it would. But it feels even worse than I thought it would.'

'Well, you know, when you ditch a perfectly good boyfriend, who doesn't want to be ditched, for no valid reason that the grapevine's managed to work out yet...' She wagged her finger, but then recognised that Christina wasn't quite up to tough love yet, even in a teasing way. 'Come and tell Auntie Grace all about it.'

Which was absurd, because Grace had to be the younger by at least five years.

They sat in the only nearby shade they could find, beneath the rainwater tank stand at the back of the little CWA building, where several pepper trees clustered. Christina fiddled with a sprig of pinkish corns, breaking them off and letting them trickle through her fingers, bringing a hot scent to her nostrils.

Normally she loved crossing the Dividing Range into this dry outback country. It was such a contrast to the steamy heat of the coast. Most people who lived in Crocodile Creek looked to the ocean—for employment, for recreation. Out here, you had the same wide horizon and yawning sky, but there was a quality of silence and stillness that brought you face to face with yourself like nowhere else.

Christina launched into the whole story—everything she loved about Joe, everything he blocked off, her decision, the thing about the room, and how she'd wanted to do this properly, make it as easy as possible on both of them, but the room had felt like a mistake, because he'd been angry about it.

'And the fact that it took us over two hours to get home from the airport didn't help.'

'What, you walked on your hands?'

She told Grace about the series of fated delays. 'I mean, they were minor. We delivered the joey to the park ranger, we fixed the tyre, we dropped the hitchhiker where he wanted to be let off. And then we got home and I couldn't put it off, because if I'd had it hanging over me until to-night, or if Joe had heard from someone else today about the room…'

Grace had questions. Had he tried to argue? Did Christina have any theories?

They finished their sandwiches and their tea, and were still talking about it.

'And I've even thought, yes, maybe he is married,' Christina said, 'but that there are mitigating circumstances so he doesn't want to tell me, even though if they were the right circumstances, I think I could…I'd try…to under-stand.'

'Yeah?' Grace made a sceptical face. 'The great myth about married men—that there can be a good excuse. Like, for example?'

'You know,' Christina's tone was self-mocking because, yes, was there ever a good excuse? 'Like his beautiful blonde wife turns into a swan during the hours of dark-ness…'

'Right.'

'And if he ever leaves her the spell becomes irreversi-ble and she's condemned to remain a swan forever. That kind of thing.'

Grace tut-tutted sympathetically. 'Yes, I've known a lot of men over the years with swan wife issues.'

'All right, all right, so I haven't been able to think of a reason I'd accept.'

'It would be a stretch,' Grace agreed. She paused, and her tone changed. 'Have you ever asked him?'

'If he's married?'

'Yes. Just straight out. "Joe Barrett, are you married?"'

'Yes, I asked him at four o'clock this morning,' Christina said bluntly. 'When we met up in the passage outside my room because neither of us could sleep.' She didn't elaborate on what had happened after that.

'And what did he say?'

'He said he wasn't.'

'But he could be lying.'

'Except that I have to believe my judgement of character is better than that!' she burst out. 'Wouldn't I know?'

'Ugh. Thousands of women in history haven't.'

'Vote of confidence there, Grace.'

'Sorry, but you were thinking it yourself, weren't you?'

'Of course I was.'

'There's more water in the flask—want the last cup?'

'No, thanks.'

They heard the chink of metal and the creak of leather and a woman came round the corner of the building, leading a horse. 'Can I tether him here?' she said. 'I'm here for the clinic. Am I early?'

'Yes, tie him up here,' Christina said. 'Is that what you usually do when you come into town?'

The woman made a face. 'I usually drive. And I don't come in often.' She looked hot and tired and driven by much more than just a need to find a place to tether her horse. 'Would there be a bucket inside? I'll need water for him, too.'

She eyed the metal tap protruding from the tank, and then the tank itself. This part of the country hadn't had much rain. Banging the flat of her hand on the corrugated iron, she listened to the sound. 'Still something in there,' she said. 'Water. That's what I'd want if I had the Midas touch, for everything to turn to water. Gold, you can keep—useless stuff!'

'I'm sure there's a bucket,' Grace said cheerfully. 'Wait right here!'

She disappeared through the back door of the building,

and the woman—she must be in her late forties, Christina thought—leaned her forehead against the satiny neck of the horse. It seemed a bit odd that Christina couldn't place her. She was clearly local, and not a new arrival. That practised way she'd banged on the water tank to judge its level by the sound suggested someone born and bred on an outback property. But Christina had been flying these clinic runs for several years and hadn't met her before.

'You'd work at the hospital sometimes, wouldn't you?' she asked Christina, after a minute. 'You'd have colleagues there?'

'Yes, we rotate the workload a lot,' Christina answered. 'I know pretty much everyone.'

'And patients? My daughter's there at the moment. Megan Cooper.'

'Oh, Megan!' The conjectures dissolved and reformed themselves in a different pattern—one which gave answers and raised new questions. 'We all know Megan. And the—' Christina stopped abruptly, horrified by what she'd almost given away.

The baby.

Little Lucky, now officially known as Jackson Cooper. Christina had filled Joe in on the dramatic story of the little boy's secret birth and miraculous survival after she'd picked him up from the airport last night, and Grace had marvelled aloud about the whole thing again during their flight this morning.

Megan was still refusing to give her consent to her parents being told about the baby's existence. Her mother—this tired woman right here, with her yearning for rain—thought that Megan had miscarried a stillborn child. The girl's father didn't even know that much. And medical ethics regarding patient confidentiality prevented any of the hospital staff from telling them.

If only the two of them could get into Crocodile Creek to see Megan, everything would surely come out in the open and the teenager's fear about her parents' reaction would recede, but the Coopers' cattle property was so crippled by drought that neither Honey nor her husband would consider making the long drive to the coast just yet. As far as they were concerned, they'd come and pick their daughter up when she was discharged, and life would go on as before.

It wasn't going to happen.

'And—and the difficult time she had,' Christina continued awkwardly, praying that Mrs Cooper hadn't noticed her gaffe. 'You must be very happy that she's doing so well now.'

'I haven't even seen her, have I? It's just…impossible, at the moment.'

'Seems like you don't travel very much.'

'Not unless we have to. I'm like a cat on hot bricks just coming this far. That's why I'm on Buckley, even though it's a two-hour ride on horseback. If I'd taken the car, Jim would have wanted to know what I was going into town for, and he would have stopped me.' She caught sight of Christina's face. 'I'm not a prisoner.' She gave a tired laugh. 'Well, I might as well be, I suppose, but it's not Jim who's keeping me in chains. It's this drought. And the work. And— Listen to me!'

Yes, I am listening to you, and I want to start treating you for depression and stress without so much as taking your blood pressure first, Christina thought. She said gently, 'Want to wait until we're comfortable inside and I've had a look at you, and tell me the rest of it then?'

'Oh, I'm not here about me, Doctor,' Mrs Cooper said. 'It's Jim, my husband.'

Grace appeared with the bucket, and the horse's needs were seen to. They were far simpler ones than Honey Cooper's, Christina realised again when she'd introduced herself properly as Dr Farrelly and asked about why Mrs Cooper was there.

'Jim won't get himself checked out,' Honey said in a weary voice. She was now seated in the little office they used for examinations and treatment. 'He had a prescription for something to keep his blood pressure down, but that's run out. Can I get another one for him if he's not here?'

'You really can't, Mrs Cooper, I'm sorry. He has to come in himself.'

'I'm cooking with less salt, like they told us at the hospital after his heart attack last year, but it's no good, because he just adds it at the table. Says he sweats too much of it out to go without. And as for the stress...! He's working too hard, his heart's in terrible shape, we know that. He's been told he should have a bypass eventually. What can I do, Dr Farrelly?'

'You have to get him to come in. I really need to see him and give him a proper check-up before I prescribe any kind of treatment, even if it is just a question of renewing prescriptions he's had before.'

Honey Cooper closed her eyes and shrugged. She was a woman who carried her burden with her wherever she went, her tortured heart right there on her sleeve.

Joe had hinted at his own burdens last night—burdens he left behind in New Zealand and was glad to escape. Christina was his temporary haven, and maybe he needed it, had the kind of problems at home that meant he deserved it, but she didn't want to be used that way any more.

She thought about prescribing a casual, part-time affair to Honey Cooper. The Joe Barrett solution.

It'll really take your mind off your troubles, Mrs Cooper. It'll do wonders for you, as a bit of R&R.

The idea was so ludicrous that she almost laughed...and then she felt angry with Joe all over again.

'Let me give you a good check-up while you're here,' she told Honey, and discovered that her blood pressure was higher than it should be, just like her husband's.

Honey's expression lightened at the news, and Christina knew quite well what would happen. The medication she prescribed for Honey would get taken by her husband instead.

'Please, try and get him to come to our next clinic,' she said as Honey rose to leave. 'Or if you can get into town over the next couple of days. Megan...' She hesitated, pulled in opposite directions by the complexity of this family's tribulations. 'Needs help working out her future,' she finished, knowing that it was inadequate and yet still probably more than she should reveal.

But Megan's mother was too weighed down by other concerns to pick up on any hints. 'Into town?' she echoed. 'Yes, when she's ready for us to bring her home.'

A high-riding four-wheel-drive pulled up at the front of the little hall as Christina ushered Honey back into the larger space that served as a waiting room. She heard a male voice over the squeak of a vehicle door whose hinges needed lubricant. 'Come on, you lot, out you get. We're late and we'll have to wait two hours at this rate.'

Honey peered out the window and froze, her renewed tension going unnoticed by Grace, who'd just called in a mother and baby for a check-up and immunisations. A couple of the other waiting patients were aware of it, however. Distances might be vast out here, but neighbours were still neighbours, and they knew each other's business.

'Philip.' A sun-weathered man in his fifties growled the greeting and stuck out his hand as the owner of the four-wheel-drive stomped confidently into the hall.

Christina knew the new arrival, although they'd only met a handful of times. Philip Wetherby. He was Charles Wetherby's younger brother, aged around forty, and he ran a huge cattle station not far from here. The two brothers weren't close—barely spoke, she gathered—but town gossip was silent as to the reasons why. Whatever the source of their grievance, it had happened a long time ago.

'Greg,' Philip said to the man who had greeted him. 'Good to see you. Your dams holding up?'

'Getting pretty low. If we don't get rain soon…'

Philip looked around the room. Honey had turned her back, and was studying some health posters pinned to the wall. His eyes fell on her but stayed blank. There was recognition, but no acknowledgement, and his gaze quickly chased through the rest of the space.

'Stupid to use this first-come-first-served system,' he said. 'I don't have time to sit around all afternoon.' He speared Christina with his impatient expression. 'Look, can't you apply some kind of triage? Lynley, my wife, had a migraine and I've had to bring these people in.' His voice dropped as his gaze flicked to the three indigenous men who'd accompanied him. They were presumably employees on the Wetherby property. 'You have to treat them like children half the time, they don't look after themselves.' He didn't wait for her agreement, just took it for granted. 'If we could get seen first…'

'I'm afraid that's not possible,' Christina replied coolly. 'As you've said, we operate on a first-come-first-served basis, unless someone needs urgent treatment.'

'My cattle need urgent treatment, but you're telling me that doesn't count.'

'Sorry.' She gave a short, polite smile then turned away from him to call her next patient.

She knew that Philip Wetherby would be fuming behind her back. Hard to believe the man was Charles's brother. Although Charles was the one with health problems, thanks to his confinement to a wheelchair, Philip looked like the weaker man—the kind who put others down in order to feel superior in his own estimation. He had a ropy build because of the physical nature of his work, but brute strength didn't equal strength of character.

Where Charles's compassionate eyes saw straight into people's hearts, Philip's critical ones took in only enough detail to give him ammunition. His mouth turned down slightly at the corners, and his top lip was too thin. You wouldn't notice it on someone you liked, someone who smiled, but on Philip Wetherby, you noticed at once.

He sat down with a grunt on the opposite side of the room to where his men had stationed themselves, and when Honey slipped out the door, he uttered an impatient snort that could have meant anything.

And even though Christina was determined not to give in to the man's I'm-too-important-to-be-sitting-here vibe, she was on edge as she saw each successive patient, and relieved when she'd dealt with the three from Wetherby Downs.

'I want you back in two weeks to see if that chest has cleared,' she told the last of them, knowing Philip Wetherby wouldn't be happy about it. Maybe he'd trust the man to get here on his own next time. Or he'd send his no doubt under-appreciated wife.

It was after four-thirty by the time she and Grace finished, having referred two patients for further tests in Crocodile Creek. They'd need to pack up their equipment quickly, as their pilot, Glenn Corcoran, would want to be in the air again within half an hour in order to get back before the light went.

Grace was in a chatty mood. Perhaps she was being kind, taking Christina's mind off Joe. 'Mrs Strachan is getting huge,' she said. 'I'm thinking she'll be early, but she said the other two have been a week late. She doesn't seem too bothered about having it at home if it jumps the gun. How did you go with the mob from Wetherby Downs? Ticked the boss cocky off, I hope.' She was talking about Philip.

'You don't like Charles's brother?'

'Do you? He's so far up himself he needs caving equipment. Which I'm sure our Charles would be happy to supply, along with a very inaccurate map.'

Christina laughed, and felt the tight fist around her heart ease its pressure just a fraction. 'You're good for me, Grace.'

'That's the plan, Chrissie. Sorry, you don't like Chrissie, do you? Or Tina?'

'Not much. Bit prissy, both of them.' Which was why Joe had soon changed Tina to Tink.

Grace dropped her voice. 'Tell me about Honey Cooper.'

'Do you know her?'

'She came to this clinic with her husband once. You must have been off that day. Who would have been doing this instead? Oh, nasty Kirsty, I suppose. The Coopers are both the type that never have a day's illness until they drop in their harness twenty years too soon. Which is about due now.'

'Grace, after that summary, I don't need to tell you a thing about Honey Cooper!'

'So why was she here?'

'For advice on her husband, who wouldn't come. They

both have high blood pressure. Jim isn't taking his underlying heart trouble seriously. His wife takes it seriously enough for both of them, but there's not a lot she can do.'

Grace shrugged. 'I could write a book on the psychology of the outback male and his partner.' She locked the cupboard where they stored a few basic supplies and surveyed the three neat rooms. 'Are we done here?'

'Looks like it.'

Mrs Considine, the CWA stalwart who ran the tiny post office and store, had closed up her premises in order to help them ferry their supplies back out to the airstrip at the edge of town, where they found Glenn frowning about a warning light on the instrument panel that was showing when it shouldn't be. He lifted hatches and checked gauges and muttered a couple of ominous phrases, then found the problem, which fortunately turned out to be an easy fix.

'Still, we've lost twenty minutes,' he said, looking at his watch.

He was a good pilot, and good at anticipating the needs of the medical personnel who flew with him, but, as Grace had said once, the sense of humour gene on the personality chromosome was missing,

'Which means he could be the best-looking man on the planet—and I'd have to say he comes close—but in my book he's about as sexy as a cardboard cereal packet.'

Christina had the same book. She spent hours with him every week, but didn't think she'd get asked to his wedding.

'What, your girlfriend can't wait that long?' Grace teased Glenn now, since she was a self-described 'woman who refused to recognise a lost cause when she fell over one'.

He raised his eyebrows and shrugged at the comment about his girlfriend, uttered a mechanical laugh since

Grace's twinkling eyes had telegraphed that he was supposed to, and went through his pre-flight routine exactly as usual.

Christina hid inside her headset and looked out the window as she waited for take-off. The late sun had begun to glow a darker gold on the rust-coloured rock and hard ground. A trail of dust boiled behind a vehicle racing along the road into Gunyamurra from the west. The town always looked so small in all this vastness, as if a giant had thrown a handful of matchboxes onto an empty table.

She tried to appreciate the grandeur of it all, to tell herself that her infinitesimal place in the universe simply didn't warrant this amount of pain in her heart about one incomprehensible New Zealander, but it didn't work.

Nothing worked today.

The dust trail from the approaching vehicle got closer. Glenn revved his engines to the moment of juddering and screaming that came just before he launched into the taxi down the airstrip, and a second later they set off, gathering ground speed rapidly. They'd shake off the earth in a few moments, and in about an hour they'd touch down in Crocodile Creek.

That vehicle and its dragging parachute of dust still nagged in the centre of Christina's vision. A service track ran parallel to the airstrip just beyond the fence, and the battered four-wheel-drive careened along it as if in a race with the plane. Crazy driver, hadn't he heard about the fatal game of chicken between two vehicles out at the Wygera settlement a week and a half ago? Racing a plane made even less sense as an adolescent game.

Then she saw that it was an older woman at the wheel, glimpsed her frantic face and manic gestures, recognised her and understood that if this was a race, it was a race for someone's life.

'Glenn!' she yelled into her headset. 'Abort take-off! Abort it now!'

CHAPTER FOUR

'ANY THOUGHTS, Joe?' Hamish McGregor said.

They stood in the tiny nursery that formed part of the obstetrics and gynaecology ward. There were two babies in it. One was a healthy, full-term girl who would go home with her mother today. She'd had a fussy night, so her mother was tired and taking a break and a nap while she could. The other baby was Jackson Cooper.

Aka Lucky.

Joe had plenty of thoughts. Not quite enough of them were about this little boy. He couldn't get last night's talk with Christina out of his head, that was the problem, couldn't believe that what they'd had was really over.

He grabbed at the mental puzzle pieces Hamish had given him. Low-grade fever, fussy and listless, not wanting to feed. Newborn babies were hard to read and important to take seriously, and this one had already endured more than his share of problems.

'It has to be an infection,' he said. 'Not at the incision, that's looking great. The cord stump is nice and dry. You said the blood and urine tests came back clear. It's just one of those non-specific things. Do everything, I'd say. IV fluids, something to bring the fever down, another course of antibiotics. Is the mother feeding him?'

'Trying to now, with some ambivalence, and they haven't got the hang of it, yet, I'm told. I won't be surprised if she chucks it in.'

'It would be really, really good if she could not chuck it in, wouldn't it?'

'You're the one with the winning smile, Joe. Convince her!'

So Joe met Megan and Jackson, the patients everyone was talking about—the ones who'd made Christina's voice go eager and soft and satisfied all at the same time last night in the car—and they had a chat, and he shamelessly ratcheted up his Kiwi accent, which often greased the wheels of conversation with Australian patients.

'Breast-feeding's the best thing for him, Megan,' he told her.

'I don't think I can.' Her sense of defeat seemed habitual.

'Yes, you can!' He crouched down beside the chair where she sat with the baby hemmed in by pillows. 'You know, with kids—with anyone you love, really, parents and siblings and friends—there are so many things that are out of your control, things you try to do for the best that can backfire. But breast-feeding's not one of them. Breast-feeding is the number one, simple, no ifs or buts or downsides, best thing you can do for your newborn baby. I'll tell you something. My mother tried so hard, but she couldn't do it for my sister.'

I'm saying too much, he realised. He was running on at the mouth. Too emotional today. Didn't quite have it all where he wanted it.

'She couldn't?' Megan said.

'My sister has some health problems.' He waved a hand, regretting that he'd gone in that direction. He hardly ever mentioned his family to a patient, let alone Amber's health. His personal life felt too close to the surface today, a professional liability. 'Point is, you can do it for Jackson, if you decide it's important to, and there are people here who'll help you with it, just a buzzer away, any time you need them.'

'There was that nice doctor…the woman…'

'Dr Farrelly?'

'No, Dr Turner. She showed me. And a nurse. I don't think she's on today. Listen, I'm not dumb, you don't need to talk down to me.'

'Sorry if it seemed that way.'

'I get what you're saying. I do want to keep trying with this, but he doesn't seem interested today, and I don't think I've got his mouth positioned right.'

'We'll find someone.' He looked at her more closely as he spoke, saw beyond the chronic air of defeat, and realised she was right. She wasn't dumb. 'Meanwhile,' he went on, 'he has a bit of a fever and he's not feeling good, that's why he doesn't seem interested. We've given him something to bring it down, and his tests have come back clear, but we're going to start him on a couple of different anti-biotics, just in case. You could also try a breast-pump, because he wouldn't have to suck so hard on a rubber teat, and sucking's too tiring for him today.'

'I get help with the breast-pump, right?'

'Yep.'

'Yip? You sound like my dog!' She actually managed a smile, and he could understand why this girl and her baby had the whole hospital community holding its breath.

'Take-off is aborted.' Glenn was still wrestling the aircraft to a controlled taxi speed, with the end of the airstrip rapidly approaching. 'Another ten metres and we couldn't have done it, Christina, do you realise that?'

'I know.' Christina's voice was shaky. She didn't mind flying, but didn't like the drama of an aborted take-off or a difficult landing.

'So this should be important.'

'I think it's going to be. That's Honey Cooper on the track beside us—Lucky's grandmother—and I don't think she's screaming after us like this just to wave us goodbye.'

Grace was craning to see as the aircraft wheeled around. 'It is Honey!' she confirmed. 'She's stopped. She's going back towards the gate. Something must have happened out at the station, and not long after she got back there from our clinic, too. With that ride, she's had a rough day, and a long one.'

'She'll want to meet us as close to the plane as she can get,' Glenn said. As everyone did around the hospital, he knew Lucky's name. 'I'll have to tell Base we've got a change of plan.' He got on the radio.

'It has to be urgent,' Christina said. 'After what she said to me this afternoon.'

'It's Jim,' Grace answered. 'I can see him there in the passenger seat beside her.' She added, more to herself than to her colleagues, 'Oh, lord, it's probably his heart again.'

It was.

The air from the propellers whipped Grace's and Christina's clothing as they ran from the plane. Honey had parked crookedly beside the end of the airstrip and opened the passenger door. Jim was slumped stiffly there, grey-faced and sweating profusely, still clearly in the grip of great pain.

He was gasping for breath, and gripping the top of his arm.

'Jim?' Christina urged him. 'Can you speak? Tell us about the pain?'

'Killing me,' he groaned. 'Help! Help me!'

'Jim, we're going to get you onto the ground.' It was dusty, but it was flat, and if they needed to start CPR…

'Why? What are you doing to him?' Honey demanded in the background. She looked as if she'd aged ten years in the past hour. 'I've got a blanket.'

'Roll it up for us, Honey.' It would help to support him in a position that made breathing easier.

'Yes… Yes.'

Glenn always seemed to know when he'd be needed, and he was there now. 'Help me get him onto the ground,' Christina said to him, and he nodded. Then to Jim, she said, 'Could you swallow an aspirin, Jim? It'll really help if you can. We're taking care of you now, and you're going to be fine.'

'I have aspirin in my bag,' Honey said, and started a panicky rummaging in a chunky, home-made leather contraption which Megan must have made for her as a child.

'Could you take it, Jim?' Christina repeated. 'Chew it up for us and swallow it down?'

He made a strangled sound which she took as a yes— *wanted* to take as a yes.

'What kind is it, Honey?' Mentally, she debated getting out their own supply, but if this was a 300 mg soluble type, and Honey had it right there, it could actually reduce the size of the infarct and make a big difference, just in the crucial window of time while their far more sophisticated equipment was brought from the plane.

Brought from the plane.

She jerked her head around too fast and found Grace. 'Grace, I want the life pack, the oxygen.' She paused for half a second while her mind raced. Suction equipment? They'd need it if the worst happened. Get Grace to bring it now, in case? She wouldn't be able to carry all that gear.

'Glenn, help her. Suction gear, medication kit. Fast, or Jim's going to think we're just slack and messing around here, aren't you, Jim?' The jokey tone didn't work, but it got her meaning across to her colleagues. 'You're doing really well, OK? We're onto this now, and you're going to be all right.'

Golden rule of heart patient treatment. Never let them think they're in trouble, even if they are, because the fear only made it worse.

She felt for Jim's pulse while Honey produced the aspirin and coaxed him to chew and swallow. It began to fizz in his mouth as it dissolved. No perceptible pulse at the wrist. That wasn't good. It meant his systolic pressure was below eighty, and she couldn't give nitroglycerine because that would only lower it further.

She found the carotid pulse in the neck and even that was weak, erratic. He was barely conscious. Telling him again that he was safe in her hands, she addressed Honey. 'Tell me about the previous trouble he's had.'

Honey's summary was confused and jumpy. It had only been a mild attack but tests had shown he should have a bypass. No, he hadn't had it yet. There just hadn't been the right chance.

'What was he doing when the pain started?'

'Seeing to the horse. Yelling at me for going into town behind his back. Turned out he'd been feeling bad all day, but he didn't tell me. If he had, I never would have left him to come to see you. To come and see you *about him*.' She gave a sob of bitter laughter at the irony.

A fatal irony, it might yet turn out to be.

Christina wasn't under any illusions here. This man was in a bad way.

Grace arrived with the portable oxygen. The cylinder

was only about fifty centimetres in length but it was still heavy. 'Want me to do it?'

'Yes. Full tilt.'

Christina's vision seemed to cloud for a moment as she spoke. Hell, was the light fading already? No, it was just the shadow from a fluffy ball of cloud, but the cloud was low in the west and while the sun floated behind it the light stayed purple and dark like a warning about the approach of dusk.

Glenn had the life kit. Christina sent him back to the plane for a stretcher, then ripped open Jim's shirt and slapped the three electrodes into place, one beneath each collar-bone and the other low on his left side roughly level with the umbilicus. She switched on the machine, saw an initial fuzz of static on the screen and then a rhythm—the wrong rhythm, the one she'd hoped not to see, with its bizarre QRS spikes indicating a complete heart block.

After getting the oxygen mask in place and the oxygen flowing, Grace wrapped a blood-pressure cuff around Jim's arm to try and get a measurement but when Christina looked at her she just shook her head.

Unreadable.

This patient could arrest at any moment.

And he was still in terrible pain.

She worked to set up an IV, needing the access for pain medication and life-saving drugs if he arrested, as she feared he would. The needle went in cleanly, followed by the plastic cannula. Grace drew up some saline to flush the line as a check, while Christina prepared morphine. With Jim's pain still at a crippling level, she gave the entire first dose at once, along with more reassurance.

'We have the drip in now, Jim, and that's going to help us medicate you and get this under control. You're going to be fine. The pain should ease very, very soon.' She added an anti-emetic to the IV because of the strong possibility that the narcotic drug would make him nauseous. 'We're going to get you into the plane now, and get you to the hospital.'

Glenn came into his own at this point, strong, adept and rock-faced. Timing their actions together, they got Jim onto the stretcher and pushed its sturdy wheels over the hard, dust-coated ground to the aircraft, while Grace took care of the equipment.

Shakily Honey asked, 'I'm coming in the plane?'

'Yes, of course.' Grace touched her arm. 'But better move the car first, Mrs Cooper.'

'Yes. Yes.' She added in a frightened tone, 'Don't— don't go without me.' She didn't trust anything right now. It wasn't rational, but it was human.

A few minutes later, Glenn launched into his pre-flight routine for the second time. Honey had left the Coopers' ancient farm vehicle parked just beyond the airstrip. She had nothing with her but the clothes she wore and that funny leather bag.

'I'm here, Jim,' she whispered to her husband, in a cracked voice. 'Jim, it's all right.'

This time their take-off proceeded without incident, and there was that sense of relief which came when the wheels had lifted and the aircraft seemed to shake off the pull of the earth. The relief was an illusion, Christina knew. There was an hour of flying to get through yet.

She barely took her eye off the ECG trace, willing it to stay in a pattern that was acceptable, if barely. Those QRS spikes were still way too wide.

Thirty minutes to go.

Twenty.

Honey hid her face against the window and silently cried. Christina could almost sense the shaking of her shoulders even when she wasn't looking in that direction. Grace comforted the woman stealthily, because no one wanted Jim to see that his wife was so upset, Honey least of all. She was doing everything she could to hide her panicky, emotional state in order to lessen her husband's own fear.

'Doing great, Jim,' Christina said. 'Nearly there now. Getting close.'

Close, but not close enough. The trace deteriorated. Ectopic beats appeared and Jim lost consciousness completely as his heart went into ventricular fibrillation, which showed on the ECG as wild, patternless wiggles. He'd gone into full cardiac arrest and his heart wasn't going to start beating again on its own.

'Glenn, we need to put down,' Christina said into her headset.

'Descent's started, Doc.'

'I can't see the coast.'

'That's because it's getting dark.'

'How far out are we? I'm really thinking we should put down.'

Was Honey listening? How much could she say about how urgent this was?

'Do we have a situation?' Glenn asked.

'Yes.' And it was against protocol to defibrillate or intubate a patient while in flight. With the powerful current in the defibrillator and the tricky technique required for intubation, it was just too dangerous, both for the patient and for the personnel working around him. CPR was possible, but less effective in the plane's confined space.

What she wanted was to drop into a level, grassy paddock in sixty seconds flat so she could work to get his heart going again, shock him and intubate, but she understood Glenn's reluctance. It was getting dark, they were just a few minutes out of Crocodile Creek, where there was a hospital, equipment, staff, even an experienced heart specialist, although not the facilities Jim would need for bypass surgery or angioplasty.

'Your call, then, Doc,' Glenn said. 'I'll find somewhere if you say we have to.'

Oh, lord, did they have to?

'Can we push up the schedule?'

'I've already requested emergency landing clearance. I can ask for a better flight path, come in faster, on a steeper descent. You won't gain much time with any of that at this point. Can't promise you'd gain much time if we drop short either, and in this light there are risks.'

'We'll go all the way,' she decided out loud. 'You'd better tell them to close the runway because we won't be getting clear of it just yet. When you're on the ground, just stop. I want the ambulance out on the tarmac right by us as soon as it's safe. Make sure they know this is happening, *stat*.'

They all felt the renewed speed and then, a little later, the steepening of Glenn's descent. He confirmed it through their headsets. 'Not long now. Bit of a pressure change coming up.'

Yes, Christina could already feel it in her ears. She swallowed, worked her jaw up and down, and felt her head clear a little. Grace began to do the same.

It was going to be a hairy landing. The seconds ticked by in slow motion, while her pulse raced and that wild electrical heart activity zig-zagged across the screen in front of her like the visual equivalent of gunfire. She had put in an airway, sliding it upside-down past the ridges on the roof of Jim's mouth and then rotating it 180 degrees to curve down over the tongue. Now she put on a bag mask and began ventilating him at twelve to fifteen breaths a minute, knowing the actions could all be futile. Handing over the bagging to Grace, she began chest compressions, struggling for effectiveness in the plane's cramped space.

'Hold his hand, Honey,' she said through her effort. 'Squeeze it and let him know you're here.'

Because you might be saying goodbye, only I don't want to tell you that.

The descent felt rough, fast and steep, and at this moment she wouldn't have exchanged any amount of a sense of humour for Glenn's steely expertise with his controls. She knew he wouldn't crack a smile at any point during this but, then, he wouldn't break a sweat either. He'd just get them onto the ground.

There was a thud and a groan as the landing gear came down. It sounded too loud and too violent, and then there came another thump, even louder, and she held her breath, terrified. If she'd pushed Glenn to make this landing too tight...

Bump. There it was, thank God, the touch of the wheels on the tarmac, crooked but not violent. A little lift came, then another bump, and they were down, careening along the runway, slowing as they went. Christina felt queasy, and Honey looked it. She still had tears squeezing from her closed eyes and her hand gripped Jim's.

As soon as their taxi speed began to feel like a car on a country road instead of an out-of-control train, Christina told Grace, 'I'll put the pads in place.'

'Your own ticker's resumed normal operations, then?' Grace said.

'You're not joking!' Christina answered. 'I was thinking just now, here we are, we're all going to die, and it's already been a *seriously* below-average day.' An unsteady sob sneaked its way into the middle of her laugh. 'It really isn't fair.'

The plane slowed...slowed...stopped. She didn't even look up to see where they were, if the ambulance had arrived, who had come with it, although she was dimly aware of Glenn skipping through most of his final procedures and jumping out onto the tarmac.

She had the pads on Jim's chest, one under the right collar-bone, the other lower down on the opposite side. The hum of the life pack charging up to 200 joules hit a crescendo then it beeped its readiness.

'Everybody clear?' she called.

Grace held onto Honey to make sure. They couldn't touch the patient or anything around him made of metal at this point. 'Yes, we're clear,' she said.

'OK, shocking now.' Christina pressed the buttons on both paddles with her thumbs to release the charge.

Jim's body jerked and the ECG trace disappeared. They waited and watched. It was like a jury sequestered before revealing its verdict. You didn't yet know the outcome. You just had to wait. Christina recharged the paddles while she did so, ready for a second shock if it was needed, and when the rhythm re-formed on the screen it was still horribly wrong.

Grace handed Honey down the aircraft steps to Glenn. There'd have to be someone on the ground to take care of her. She needed it at this point. What she didn't need was to witness any more of this.

'Shocking again at 200,' Christina said as soon as Honey had gone and the charge had built again.

No go.

'And again at 360.'

No.

She felt movement—a vibration and some thumps as someone entered the plane. In the warm tropical air of the coast, she hadn't even realised the rear door had been opened.

'How long since he arrested?' Oh, lord, it was Joe! She would have known it in another second even without hearing his voice, just by the aura of his body next to hers, just by the way he smelled.

Flooded with an impossible mix of emotion—relief… way too much of it was relief…just that physical relief she always felt at being with him, like an addict getting a drug—she answered, 'I've lost track. Too long. They sent you from the ED with the ambulance?'

'Yes. You've shocked up to 360?' He leaned closer and she felt his solid upper arm brush hers, bare beyond the short sleeve of the surgical scrub suit he wore. The sensation was so familiar, but it didn't belong to her any more.

He didn't belong to her.

He never had.

'Yes,' she answered, after drawing in a breath. 'I'm going with adrenaline and I'm going to intubate. CPR and bag him for a minute, just to get some air and circulation pushing through.'

'Then shock him again…'

'Yes.' If his heart hadn't produced a rhythm by then… Well, you still kept going, another cycle of three shocks followed by CPR, you tried everything for thirty or forty minutes, and you watched for the miracle, but the chance of it got less and less.

Grace was already drawing up the adrenaline. Joe

started CPR, pausing only long enough for Christina to intubate with Grace's help.

'OK, standing clear, please. Shocking now at 360 joules.'

Jim's body jumped again. The trace went static, then a rhythm resolved.

'Sinus pattern,' Joe said.

'Thank God for that!'

'Forty. It's too slow.'

'I'll give atropine.'

'Hopefully it won't come up too far or we'll be back where we started.'

'We?' Every muscle in her body tightened. 'It's not *we*, Joe. Don't use that word, please.'

Oh, hell, where had that come from? Unprofessional and stupid and just wrong. She set her face hard, willing herself to forget the rash personal reference, and willing him to ignore it.

He did, and Christina hardened her control so that she didn't risk letting down the barriers again.

She drew up the dose, hoping it wouldn't speed the heart up too fast and send it once more into the wild electrical rhythm that couldn't translate into the right beat. Unfortunately, a patient's reaction to the drug couldn't be predicted.

'OK,' Joe said a few minutes later. 'Looking better, now. He's up to sixty.'

'Gag reflex is back. I'm taking out the airway.'

'Give him the high-oxygen mask and see how he goes.'

They watched and waited. Jim stirred and groaned through his mask, his depth of unconsciousness lightening. They would be able to move him soon.

'Who else do we have on the ground?' Christina asked.

'Ambulance and two officers, one is driving, one's with

the patient's wife. That's Nick Brady. You'd know him, he's pretty good. She seems…'

He stopped, tilted his head in the direction of the tarmac and listened. Christina heard voices, but didn't take her eyes from the heart monitor. Joe leaned out the door and came back half a minute later to report quietly, 'She's done a bit of a dive.'

Christina made a stricken sound. She knew Honey must be on the edge of a complete nervous collapse.

'Nick doesn't think it's serious.' That was partly for Jim's benefit, Christina knew, because it was just possible that he could hear and take in what was going on. 'Low blood sugar, exhaustion, stress. But they're going to send for a second ambulance and check her out.' He dropped his voice even lower. 'What do we know about these two?'

He'd said it again.

We.

Such a little word, but it hurt so much, the way it mocked their current status.

Christina ignored it and just answered the question. 'Patient is Jim Cooper, Megan's father. Remember, I told you last night about—'

'Right.' He gave a short, efficient nod, which made his jaw look very strong and square, and murmured, 'I got introduced to Megan and the bub today.'

Grace—who must be aware of the undercurrents—leaned closer to Christina and said, 'Speaking of which, there's a family reunion coming up. Thought about that yet, Christina?'

'Uh…' Lord, no! She hadn't! In the few moments when she hadn't been focused purely on the technical demands of Jim's care, she'd been thinking about a very different reunion. Her own, just now, with Joe. Which had been every bit as difficult as she'd known it would be.

But Grace was right. Honey would want to see Megan as soon as she could, once she'd regained her own strength a little and satisfied herself that Jim was stable. And when Honey saw Megan, she would see her new grandson as well, unless they called ahead to the unit and got an express refusal from Megan to allow her mother through the door. Would the girl go that far? Would Honey take any notice?

'Let's take it one step at a time,' Christina answered. 'For now, for us, this is just about Jim.'

'You think so? Tell you what, we'll swap jobs for to-night,' Grace murmured back, smiling wryly. 'I'll do the life-saving and you can clean up the family mess.' She was a good enough friend to get away with the challenge.

Christina said, 'You're saying it's going to get dumped on you?'

'I'm saying nurses have the sticky bits sometimes. I'm not looking forward to it, because if it gets stuffed up somehow and they all end up permanently estranged...'

'They'd all lose out,' Joe cut in, as if he knew something about such a prospect.

'And I'll feel to blame,' finished Grace.

'Don't, Grace,' Joe said. 'Whatever's going on, it must have started months ago, before anyone at this hospital was ever involved.'

Grace nodded. 'You're right, of course. But feelings don't operate on logic, do they?'

'Heck of a lot easier if they did.' He looked tired and stressed suddenly.

The skin around his big, dark eyes was tight, and his hair stuck up at the back as if he'd run his hand through it too many times since its morning brush. Christina wondered what kind of a day he'd had, what kind of a month he'd just come from in New Zealand, what kind of a *life* he had there, for heaven's sake, and how much work he'd put in to settle into his room in the doctors' house this morning.

She'd done most of it for him yesterday, of course. Made the bed, hunted up the books, picked those flowers. Had she tried too hard? Said too much, with all these gestures?

Stop.

Just stop.

'Heart rate up to sixty-five, respirations are coming up, too,' she said. 'I think we should move him now. We've been hogging this runway long enough.' She changed her tone a little and spoke directly to Jim, even though he still hovered on the edge of unconsciousness. 'We're going to get you into a hospital bed now, Jim, where we have some better machines for reading what's going on with your heart. We'll give you something more for the pain before we go.'

He could take another dose of morphine at this point, she judged. When she'd delivered it through the port in his IV she asked him how he was doing and was rewarded with the flickering of his closed lids and the faintest nod.

The transfer to the ambulance went well. An onlooker wouldn't have sensed any drama, or any frantic hurry. Still, the danger wasn't over, and possibly the journey wasn't either, if he needed to go south for the kind of surgery they weren't equipped for here.

The hospital seemed quiet as they turned into the ambulance bay, a reassuring edifice with its modern design and clean lines. Glimpsing the waiting room that opened off the emergency department entrance, Christina saw two or three patients waiting, and there were lights in the windows of the main building, of course. If you looked closely, you could glimpse a couple of TV screens. Darkness had fallen while they had been working over Jim on the airport tarmac, and from somewhere she could smell hot, savoury food.

A quick, smooth journey along a corridor brought them to a bed in the resuscitation section of the ED. Honey had been given a bed of her own in the adjacent area of the unit. She was in the care of a nurse and Christina saw she'd been hooked up to a drip. She had a cup of tea in her hands also, but hadn't made much headway with it.

She reacted as soon as she saw them, struggling to sit higher and breaking into rapid speech. 'I'm sorry. This is so stupid. I don't need this. Jim, I'm here,' she called, 'but they've got me in a bed. Can I bring this thing with me?' She gestured, impatient and agitated, towards the drip stand.

The nurse raised her eyebrows in a question and Christina and Joe both nodded. Honey would only fret herself into a worse state if she couldn't get closer to her husband. Grace took over, helping her out of bed and making sure her IV line wasn't wrapped around her. 'This way, Mrs Cooper.'

'We're going to put him on a better ECG machine,' Christina explained. 'It has more leads, which might feel a bit scary, Jim, all these things stuck to you, but it's only so we can work out what kind of heart attack you've had. We'll be taking some blood as well, giving you more medication through your drip and monitoring you very closely.'

We.

She was doing it now, too.

It was the way medical personnel often talked. Safety in numbers, or something. But until last night 'we' had meant something much more personal in a context like this. Herself and Joe, working together, understanding each other, getting the team-work right, feeling good about what they did because they knew they did it well…

Then planning a night out afterwards. A crazy night sometimes. Mad races along the beach, kicking up the foam with their bare feet. Lighting a campfire in the back garden and toasting kebab sticks threaded with marshmallow, banana and pineapple pieces, then dipping them in melted chocolate.

Filling a kid's wading pool on a hot summer night once, and setting up the television and video player on the back veranda in front of it because Joe had said, 'Hey, feel like a naked spa movie marathon?' They'd both been pretty inventive when it had come to making entertainment. They'd had so much fun.

Yes.

Fun.

Rest and recreation, just the way Joe had wanted.

Focus, Christina.

She was supposed to be taking blood.

Now.

Because they needed to measure the cardiac enzymes to get a definitive marker of infarct size. They'd get a result within minutes and a clearer answer on whether they would need to ship him south to Brisbane for surgery, and what medication he should be given in the interim.

Honey watched them like a hawk as they worked to set up the ECG and take the blood. Jim opened his eyes as the needle went in.

'Hey, you're back with us,' Joe said. 'I'm Dr Barrett—Joe, if you want—and you're safe here in Crocodile Creek Hospital, Mr Cooper. We're going to take good care of you.'

'Are you in much pain now, Jim?' Christina asked him. The thin plastic cannula began to fill with blood as she spoke, and it was flowing nicely. Wouldn't take long to fill the test tubes.

'Much better,' Jim managed to reply, his voice thin.

'Oh, Jim!' Honey bowed her head and pressed his hand between hers. Her IV tubing snaked across his arm.

'Tracing's looking a lot better, too,' Joe said quietly. He drew Christina further away from the bedside, into the adjacent and almost empty section of the department. 'What are you thinking? I guess technically he's my patient now, but you probably want to follow through.'

'What I'm thinking? It's definitely an inferior infarct and the pain's settling already, so that's good. We'll see what the enzyme levels are like and start thrombolysis. Hopefully the ECG changes will settle and we won't have to transfer him for more invasive treatment. We'll get Dr Lopez to see him, discharge…' She stopped.

'Cross that bridge later.'

'I'm too tired to iron out all their family and financial problems tonight, that's for sure.'

'I'm going to have a better look at his missus, but it seems best to keep her in overnight, too,' Joe said. 'She's looking a wreck.'

'What time do you get off?' The question slipped out of Christina's mouth all by itself, pure habit.

She saw him stiffen. 'Hamish is on tonight,' he said. 'He's in here already, in Paeds, pretty busy with a couple of sick kids. Lucky spiked a fever this morning, by the way, but we couldn't find a specific problem and he seems much better now. I'll go when Hamish tells me things have quietened down, but I'm on call, so if things get hairy… Did you want—?'

'I didn't want anything,' she cut in quickly. 'I was just asking.'

'Because I do want to talk,' he told her.

He bent his head, only moving a few inches closer with the gesture but still it had the effect of locking out the rest of the world and flooding her with all her painful awareness of him. How could she ever get used to this? To being close to him without touching, to hearing his voice when the words weren't meant only for her, to pretending to him and herself and everyone else that this was OK, they were friends, they were fine, she wasn't breaking apart inside.

'Tonight?' she said, wanting it and dreading it at the same time.

He was so big. Like a wall. She had to look down, inspect her fingernails for life-threatening cuticle splits or something, because anywhere else she looked she'd only see his body, his face, his eyes.

And even when she didn't look, she could still feel.

'I know we're both tired,' he said. 'Maybe it's a mistake. But there were a couple of things you said. A couple of things I should probably say. Not feeling that patient about waiting.'

'I'm not sure, Joe.'

'Will you be home?' he pressed.

She nodded. There was nowhere else she wanted to be.

Not that she wanted to be at home much either, when her place would seem so...so...

Joe-less.

Oh, hell!

'So when I'm done here, or even if I'm only grabbing a break, I'll be over.' His voice rumbled in his chest and she wanted to do what she'd done so many times in the past and press her ear there—half her body, really—so she could feel the vibration. 'It might be late.'

'All right,' she answered.

'There are some things I want you to understand, even

though they won't change anything about…what you've said.'

It sounded ominous, not something to look forward to.

But she looked forward to it all the same, because as he turned to go back to their patient and she got slammed yet again with all the familiarity of his body—the way he moved, the shape of him—she knew she wouldn't forgive herself if she didn't give him—give herself?—just one more chance.

CHAPTER FIVE

'CHRISTI-I-I-NA! How goes it?' said the hospital administrator.

'Hi, Brian.'

She didn't like the way he said her name, or his frequent jaunty mannerisms with his voice. Having left a much more stable and comfortable Jim and a resting Honey in the care of Joe and a nurse in the emergency department, she'd gone in search of Grace before leaving the hospital for the evening—and she hoped Charles Wetherby might be around, too—but maybe Grace had already gone. The two of them were both overdue to clock off, after a longer than usual day.

Unless Grace had gone to see Megan and the baby.

Heading that way, Christina had had to pass Brian Simmons's office and he'd caught sight of her, unfortunately. She always felt petty in her response to him. He seemed like a perfectly decent guy, had helped her more than he'd really needed to over the business of organising the room in the doctors' house for Joe.

He shouldn't rub her up the wrong way just because of a few irritating mannerisms, which were no doubt designed to disguise a level of insecurity and unhappiness in his personal life that she should feel an extra dose of empathy for today.

In a warmer tone, she added, 'What are you still doing here at this time in the evening? You can't be doing emergency surgery on a file folder.'

'You see, that's what everyone thinks—that because it's not immediately about saving lives, my job fits neatly into nine till five,' he said seriously. 'But Jill and I have been sweating over staffing and budget issues for the past two hours.' He dropped his voice. 'Bit of TLC, too, to be honest, but don't let that go any further, will you? Jill hates to have her private life splashed around.'

'Of course, Brian.'

Over his shoulder, Christina could see the director of nursing seated at the desk. The light from the lamp there struck the far side of her face, while the near side, in shadow, was tear-stained. She had a mature, maternal kind of beauty in the uneven lighting, but she didn't look happy.

Brian followed the direction of Christina's gaze, but didn't say anything for a moment. 'I'm glad I can count on you,' he finally replied quietly. 'Her ex-husband should be shot and dumped in the concrete for the new bridge, I'm telling you.'

He almost looked ready to do the deed himself.

Was something going on between the two of them? Christina had always found Jill Shaw uncomfortably frosty and rigid, but if Brian, of all people, had seen something else—something sadder—beneath the surface of her personality, something that reflected a dark truth about the marriage she'd ended last year...

He *was* a kind person in his way. Observant. There was more to him than the awkward, pompous bean-counter that first met the eye.

'I'll leave you to it,' Christina said, and actually found herself patting him on the arm.

Her emotions were on a hair trigger today. She knew Brian's wife had left him several years ago. It must have hurt a lot. She understood the hurt now, in a raw, physical way she wouldn't have quite known about before.

'No, it's fine, we're done. Jill?' he called back into the office. 'You're not still pushing those numbers around, I hope. I told you to go. Come in for a minute, Christina,' he invited her. 'Give me an update on tonight's admission.'

But when Jill had picked up her bag, acknowledged Christina in her usual distant way and hurried off, Brian didn't seem all that interested in Jim Cooper after all.

'Look, I know you must be having a tough week,' he said. 'I've been through it myself and, believe me, I know. The emptiness. Thoughts going round and round. Wrong-headed solutions. You shouldn't sit at home. Can I twist your arm and march you out of the house on, say, Wednesday or Thursday night for a meal?'

'Oh, Brian, I don't—'

'Very low-key and casual. Just between friends. Work colleagues who have more in common than they did a week ago. That's all.'

She didn't want to go. Not with Brian. Not with anyone, really. He was right. She dreaded going home tonight, but once she got there she knew she'd just want to sit and let her thoughts circle in her head, not make the effort to go out again. She wasn't so sure about the 'wrong-headed solutions'.

Sitting at home all week would be wrong-headed, though, wouldn't it? Knowing Joe was in town, but that they weren't together even in the hours he wasn't working? Just thinking about it, about him, with nothing new to conclude?

Lord, she felt as if she was getting flu. Her whole body ached with the effort of holding everything together.

And Brian had been through it, too.

'As long as it's low-key,' she said. 'Pizza or burgers in town. That'd be good. But I'm not up for a big evening.'

'Did I mention a big evening? Let's rewind the tape.' He pretended to listen. 'Nope. Definitely no mention of a big evening.'

She had to laugh. 'All right, then. Thursday?'

Because that would give Joe three whole days to realise how blind he was, and if she and Joe were doing something together, of course Brian would understand if she cancelled their—

Stop it, Christina!

'Thursday. Great. It's in the diary. Pick you up at seven?'

'Sounds good.' She heard sounds coming through the rather thin wall between this office and that of Charles Wetherby, next door. 'Charles is still around?' she asked.

'Is he ever not?'

'Well, true. I'm going to grab him while I can, anyhow.'

'Always happy to be grabbed,' the medical administrator said a minute later, when Christina had apologised for doing it.

She apologised again when she tried to outline Honey Cooper's request, made at a desperate gabble just before Christina had left the ED. 'I'm sorry, it sounds unnecessarily complicated, doesn't it?'

'Contact Mrs Considine-at-the-Gunyamurra-store's nephew's brother-in-law, because the nephew himself is away, but Mrs Considine has to phone the brother-in-law because Honey doesn't have the number, and Mrs Considine has cards at Fiona Donnelly's on Monday nights so you'd have to chase her up there, and Honey does have

the number for the Donnellys,' Charles parroted, propel-
ling his wheelchair towards a file cabinet. 'Just a little bit
complicated, if I've even got it right.'

'Which is why I thought it might be a lot easier if you
could phone Wetherby Downs and ask someone from there
to go over.'

'Right,' Charles said, with his back to her.

His back communicated a lot.

A deep-seated reluctance, for one thing.

Christina apologised again. She'd known there were
long-standing family tensions, but she also knew that
Wetherby Downs was a huge property. There'd be a man-
ager. She could make the call herself and speak to him, if
Charles could give her the number. He would suggest this
himself, surely, if he didn't want to speak to his brother in
person.

'Honey isn't in good shape,' she said, pleading her case,
wishing she'd just gone with the nephew's brother-in-law's
et cetera. 'Aside from the anxiety, she was dehydrated,
low blood sugar, underlying high blood pressure. Just exhausted, basically. She's fretting because she doesn't know
if Jim let the cow and calf out or if they're stuck in the shed
with no water and feed, and then there are the dogs. I
promised I'd make sure that someone—'

'The Considine brother-in-law whose phone number
we don't have.'

'Yes, or whoever I could get—would go over to the
Coopers' and check that everything was OK.'

Charles spun around silently in the wheelchair. He was
good at that, athletic and adept. Once his lower body
strength would have matched the powerful build of his
arms and torso, and he'd probably ridden a horse as if he'd
been born on a saddle.

'No, it's about time I talked to Philip, actually,' he said, on a controlled sigh. 'Let's not go on this wild-goose chase with the Considine brother-in-law's whoever. I'll phone my brother and he'll send someone. You can tell Honey and Jim it's taken care of.'

'Thanks, Charles, I know it's probably an errand you don't need.'

'Might be an errand a few people *do* need,' he murmured, adding, 'Get yourself off home, if you're doing clinic hops again tomorrow.'

'Is he going to die, Dr Barrett?' Honey reached up from the hospital bed and clutched Joe's arm, her voice an agonised whisper. Jim lay just metres away beyond the door into the resus area.

'No, he's not going to die, Mrs Cooper.' He felt much more confident in saying it now.

The first lot of bloods had come back—more would be taken at intervals during the night—and they looked good, as did his ECG tracing. It apparently hadn't been the massive infarct that it could have been, given the drama. He was on a barrage of medication, and it was working.

'What's going to happen, then?'

Joe outlined the best-case scenario. 'We'll keep him in here for a few days, on continuous monitoring and treatment. If everything has resolved well, he can go home and he can even build his activity levels back up pretty much to where they were, as long as he feels comfortable. But he'll need more treatment. A scheduled procedure—a bypass or angioplasty—will give you both a chance to make preparations. You've been told about that in the past, I understand.'

'We just haven't been able to manage it,' Honey answered.

'Well, you'll have to manage it soon. There's still a chance he may need the surgery on a more urgent basis but, from what I'm seeing so far, I'm cautiously optimistic that he won't.'

'Oh! Oh, that's wonderful!' She blinked back tears. 'Is he sleeping?'

'Dozing.'

'I want to see my daughter. I don't know where she'd be. Which ward, I mean.'

'Want me to check for you?' Joe asked.

He knew quite well that Megan was in the obstetrics and gynaecology unit with her baby. He also knew that she didn't want to see her parents. He got the impression that no one would be too upset if Honey somehow managed to get up there on her own and thus forced the issue. But he wanted to make sure.

He went to the phone at the nurses' station and dialed the extension for O and G.

Got Christina.

'Tink?' he said automatically, and felt his stomach lurch sideways. 'What are you doing on this phone?'

'Joe? What's happened? I'm just, you know, hovering. Are you still in the ED?'

'Yes. Everything's fine. ECG tracing has improved a bit more. Bloods came back and look good.' He reported the figures. 'But Mrs Cooper wants to see her daughter. How are we handling that?'

Silence.

'I think we're not,' she finally said. 'I think it's going to be an "oops". Is that playing God?'

'Probably. But, hey, I was born for the role.'

She laughed, then said, 'Don't, Joe.'

And he knew what she meant.

Don't remind me how much we always laugh when we talk.

'Actually, Megan's having a rest now and Lucky's in the nursery,' she said. 'That might be a good thing. The two of them can talk, and—Yes, tell Honey that Megan's in Room Four.'

Grace raised her eyebrows when Christina put down the phone. 'We're letting it happen?'

'How are we going to stop it? Honey's not the type to nod politely and do nothing if she's told, "I'm sorry, your daughter has asked us not to let you see her." We're not a prison, and she's not a danger to the patient.'

'You don't know that,' Grace said, in a voice of doom.

'I do know that! They're going to kill themselves in that family, not each other!' Deliberately, she went over to Megan's bed and touched her shoulder, knowing that Grace would be watching her every move. 'You've got a visitor coming, love,' she said.

Megan's eyes opened sleepily, then went wide. 'Is it—?' She stopped. 'Who?'

'Your mum.'

'Mum? *Mum?* She—'

'Talk to her. She's had a rough day.' Briefly, Christina outlined what had happened to Megan's dad, stressing that his condition looked as if it would resolve well. 'Jackson's in the nursery, and we'll keep him there for now,' she finished. 'How you handle it is up to you.'

'Oh, he's beautiful, Megan! Just beautiful!'

After a tearful ten minutes of talking between mother and daughter, Honey held her new, sleeping grandson in her arms. He still looked frail and small following the heart surgery he'd needed shortly after birth. He'd had a spike of fever that morning—Christina and Grace were glad they hadn't heard about it until a short while ago—but this had resolved with IV fluids and medication.

'You're not angry?' Megan said.

Honey made a helpless sound. 'How could I be angry?'

'Dad was, six months ago. I thought he was going to kill Jack, and he didn't even know about the baby.'

'Does Jack know about the baby, love?'

'No. He's gone. I thought he might write, but—I guess he took Dad pretty seriously, and then when they sacked him over at Wetherby Downs… I *hate* Philip Wetherby! We're not going to tell Dad about the baby, OK?'

'Oh, love…'

Seated at the nearby nurses' station, Grace and Christina looked at each other. It was impossible not to overhear. Mother and daughter's voices rose as their conversation grew more heated, and there was no other noise in the unit. The second mother and baby who'd been in Megan's room today had gone home, and a couple of Georgie Turner's gynae patients across the corridor had their TV sound systems pressed close to their ears.

'Don't sound like that,' Megan said. 'Don't talk as if I'm being unreasonable. Mum, you are the one who's said all along that we can't upset Dad, and what could possibly upset him more than this?'

'The baby's so beautiful…'

'But that doesn't solve anything!' she burst out. The baby in Honey's arms didn't stir. 'You can't act as if we're all happy families now. People keep treating me as if I'm dumb. I'm not. We're going to lose the farm because I'm not bringing Jackson back out there, hours from a doctor when he's had all this trouble, when he so nearly died, and you and Dad can't manage the place without me. Unless we get a hundred millimetres of rain, like, *tomorrow,* he's the last straw.'

'Megan—'

'Yes! My baby is breaking the camel's back right now, today, this week. I could have given him up. I thought about it. But I made the choice. And I knew what I was doing. I've chosen my baby over the farm. We can't have both, in this drought. And I don't think Dad will ever forgive me for that.'

'He'll have to be told—'

'Yes!' Megan agreed fiercely. 'Of course he'll have to know eventually! But let me get out of this hospital and settled here in town first before we talk to Dad. Let his heart get better before I break it again.'

She glared at her mother, ready for a counter-attack. None came. Honey's head was bent over the little bundle in her arms. Their drip bags and drip stands—one adult-sized, one for an infant—stood behind them like sentinels.

'She's upset,' Grace murmured, frowning at Honey. 'She doesn't need this. She's supposed to be a patient herself tonight.'

'I'll take her back to the ED.'

'Are they going to try and find a ward bed for her?'

'She doesn't want one. They're keeping Jim in Resus overnight, and she wants to stay close. No one's arguing.' Against Honey's desire to stay with Jim, Christina meant.

'Except these two,' Grace answered, meaning something different.

'Yes, and you're right, they've done enough of it tonight.' She stood up and went to Honey. 'Let's get you some rest now, Mrs Cooper.'

Honey looked up and nodded, her cheeks wet with tears.

'Megan, can I give Jackson to you?' Christina asked,

and Megan held out her arms at once. They transferred the delicate baby carefully, and he didn't waken.

Honey got to her feet and Christina helped her twitch the IV tubing out of the way. 'We'll sort this out,' she promised her daughter, but it was obvious that she didn't have any answers. 'Twenty-six years!' she said as they walked along the corridor in the direction of the ED. 'Twenty-six years ago this mess started, Dr Farrelly. Who would have thought it would end up this way?'

'I don't know the story,' Christina told her.

'No, of course you don't. It was all kept pretty quiet. It's wrong when that happens. After all, it was an accident. All three of them agreed on that. You still don't know what I'm talking about, of course.'

'No, I'm sorry, I don't.'

'Charles and Philip and my Jim. It happened just after he and I started seeing each other, but he wouldn't listen to any advice of mine about how to handle what went on. The three of them were out pig-shooting. Jim and Charles were eighteen, but Philip was five years younger, only a kid. And Jim made a mistake and shot Charles, and old man Wetherby never forgave him for it. Wouldn't even believe it was an accident at first, because at one stage Jim and Charles were after the same girl. Wetherby cut off our access to Gunya Creek at the crossing. The Coopers had had an agreement over the creek water with the Wetherbys for sixty years. After the old man died, Jim went to Philip—he was running the property by then; Charles was still finishing his medical degree—and asked him, *begged* really, to give the access back, but Philip said no. It had only ever been a favour by the family in the past, and he was under no obligation. Since then...' She stopped and shook her head, too weary to go on, but Christina didn't need to hear any more.

'That's why Charles is in a wheelchair? Because Jim shot him?'

'Yes. All three of them weren't taking the right care. They never told me a story that made complete sense. Philip was mucking around, Charles was distracted. There was blame on all sides, Charles admitted that himself. Old man Wetherby thought it had ruined Charles's life, but he was a stronger man than that and he's made something of himself. Wetherby should have been proud of his eldest son, but Philip was always the golden boy for him. I know Charles hasn't had much to do with any of them since.'

Christina didn't know what to say. She finally blurted, 'Who knows about this?'

'Oh, a lot of people. Word gets around. It's no secret in Gunyamurra. But it's an old story now. Jim can be…difficult sometimes. He's too proud for his own good. He doesn't rally the support some men might get in his position. He had a pretty rough upbringing. I think I'm the only person who ever sees…' She tried again. 'Even Megan doesn't see…' She couldn't go on.

They reached the emergency department, and when he heard the sound of their approach, Jim opened his eyes. 'Honey,' he breathed, then closed his eyes again and was immediately asleep.

Outside, the night air was still warm, although a breeze from the ocean made it feel fresh.

Hometime, Christina thought.

Collect her car and house keys from the main desk in the ED, where Joe had said he'd leave them, collect her car from one of the reserved staff spaces where he would have parked, and drive home.

Something to eat. Water the plants. Check for phone

messages. Open her wardrobe and move the hangers along to fill the empty space where Joe's shirts had been until today. While dealing with the wardrobe, decide what she'd wear for her low-key dinner with Brian on Thursday night, because she hadn't done laundry for over a week and there might not be many clean options left.

She couldn't do it.

She couldn't go out with Brian, not even on the terms he'd proposed, not when the thought of Joe's missing shirts had twisted inside her like a rusty knife-blade. She should never have said yes.

Turning, she went back into the hospital foyer and headed in the direction of the hospital administrator's office. If he was still there, she'd tell him face to face. If he wasn't, she'd leave a note.

His light was on, she found, and his door was open. Apparently he was still in the building somewhere. Not wanting to be discovered in the act of cowardly note-scribbling, she waited, and realised that Charles was still there also, in his office just beyond the thin, inadequately sound-proofed wall.

He was on the phone.

'Tell me why I shouldn't despise you, Philip,' she heard. 'You had the perfect opportunity to end all this after Dad died. You told me you would. I thought you had. I never realised it had become so dire.'

There were some seconds of silence. Christina didn't know what to do. She peered out into the corridor, but there was still no sign of Brian. Charles's office door was tightly closed. She found a pad of sticky notes, tore the top one off, wrote 'Dear Brian,' and stood with the pen poised over the little yellow square while her mind stayed blank as to what to put next.

'Your standing in the community?' Charles said, in the adjacent office. 'That's—' Silence again, then, 'Yes, of course I accept my share of the blame. Dear God, we were kids, all three of us. Look, we're going to do something about this, and we're going to talk again. For now, you're telling me you couldn't have fathered this child but, to be honest, Philip, your word may not be good enough for me at this point.'

She couldn't stay any longer, Christina realised. Charles was so private about his personal life and his family history. He would never be talking like this if he knew he could be heard. And she couldn't write the note for Brian. The right, appropriate, carefully censored words just wouldn't come, while tears—along with all the wrong words—threatened to come all too easily.

Dear Brian, I've realised I can't go out with you on Thursday night. I'm still so in love with Joe that it feels like an illness. I'm hungry, but my stomach has shut down and gone queasy. I'm exhausted, but I know I'm going to lie awake all night. I know I've done the right thing, but in many ways that only makes it worse. Sorry. We'll reschedule in three years, when I'm cured.

She crumpled up the yellow scrap with 'Dear Brian' on it, shoved it in her trouser pocket, slipped out of the office and faced the prospect of her empty home.

CHAPTER SIX

As it turned out, Christina's house wasn't empty.

Or rather, her wide front veranda wasn't.

Joe was waiting for her, warm and solid, taking her in his arms as soon as she'd taken the steps that led up from the garden to the raised floor level. 'Sorry if I scared you,' he said.

'You didn't,' she admitted. 'I'd been thinking you might be here.' She pushed him gently away and he let her do it. The warmth he'd created on her skin lingered there, however.

'And I thought you definitely would be,' he said. 'I got a lift with Georgie Turner. She drove off and then I found a light on inside, but no one here.'

'I left the light on this morning, in case I got back after dark. And, Joe, you know where I keep the spare key.'

Silence.

'It didn't feel right,' he finally said.

And, yes, he was right, it didn't, not after he'd given her back his own key to the house just that morning.

'Well, I'm here now,' she said on a slight edge. 'It's safe for you.' She unlocked the front door and they went inside, their tension with each other more evident the moment they were in an enclosed space.

'What, should I really just have let myself in, Christina?' he asked, dropping his voice low. 'I'm not living here any more.'

He prowled around the living room. They both did, too ill at ease to sit or do anything logical like eat or pour a drink. It felt so weird and wrong and impossible, the fact that she couldn't just go up to him and hug him anymore, stroke his face. It slashed her confidence to the roots at one stroke. The rights you had over someone else's body when you were together, the blurring of space—she just hadn't realised it would feel so weird and so terrible when those rights were gone.

She was the faithful type. She'd known that about herself for years. Ending their relationship didn't mean she'd switched off her feelings. She'd go on loving Joe Barrett for a long time.

'Have you eaten?' he suddenly asked.

'Uh…'

'Because you look pale. I haven't either, but I bet I had more today than you did. Can we find something? Or get pizza, or something?'

'I don't want pizza,' she answered quickly.

Pizza was too cosy, too casual and sexy. Pizza was what they'd done too many times before when they'd been tired. Pizza you ate with your fingers, leaning over the coffee-table, and you watched a movie together, you didn't have some challenging 'talk' while dealing with strings of melty cheese. She loved watching Joe eat, because he had the perfect combination of mess and grace and relish, but she didn't want to watch him eating pizza tonight.

She was still thinking about it when he disappeared into the kitchen. She followed him. 'What are you doing?'

'Scrambled egg on toast. We'll bung some bacon in the sandwich press if there is any.'

He was using 'we' again. The really nice, casual 'we' that in the past had meant impromptu picnics on the carpet or fruitless fishing trips or lazy sessions in bed.

'Tell me what you wanted to talk about, Joe.'

'Not until I've got some food into you.' He was already cracking the eggs into a bowl. He pulled a wooden chair out for her at the kitchen table. 'Sit, OK?'

She did, but only because she'd begun to wonder how much longer her legs would hold her up, and whether her empty stomach would stay where it belonged. Time slowed and her will-power went walkabout. She sat there and watched him work and made no attempt to control anything about the situation.

He looked at her occasionally, as if to check that she hadn't slumped onto the table, but he didn't speak, just forked the eggs until the yolks and whites mixed, dropped bread into the toaster, heated the sandwich press and sliced the rinds off bacon.

'How come you're like this, Joe?' she blurted out when the meal was almost ready. 'So protective?'

'Is that not masculine enough, or something?'

'No, I didn't mean that. The opposite, in some ways. A lot of way less masculine men than you just don't know how to take care of anyone but themselves. My Dad.' Her parents lived hundreds of kilometres south, on the Gold Coast. They'd never met Joe. Which said something. 'I love my dad, but his idea of taking care of my mother when she's tired is to tell her it's OK if she's ten minutes late getting dinner on the table.'

He shrugged. 'Different generation.'

'It's not just that. You see, you never talk. Any time I

give you a cue to tell me about your life at home, your childhood, what's made you who you are, any of that, you head it off and turn it into a generalisation.'

'I said I wanted to talk tonight, didn't I?' On the face of it, it sounded like a belligerent, confrontational line, but it wasn't when Joe said it. It still contained the same easy-going flavour, the tiny nuance of a tease. He put down the two plates of eggs and bacon on toast, and brought a jug of water and a carton of orange juice to the table.

'Yes,' she said aggressively, not feeling easygoing at all. 'So talk.'

So talk.

Joe cut off an egg-piled corner of his toast and forked it into his mouth, buying time. He already knew that he wasn't going to be any good at this. He'd spent too much time training himself in that direction. He didn't believe that talking could change anything, and yet he'd been the one to suggest it. Nice contradiction, Dr Barrett! Why had he decided that Christina needed to know all of this stuff about his life?

To be fair, I guess, he decided inwardly.

Life hadn't been all that fair to the Barretts, but this didn't mean he had to continue the family tradition.

'My sister has Treacher Collins syndrome,' he said. He hadn't planned such a dramatic opening line, but it had come out all by itself, prompted by the life's-not-fair thing, probably.

'Treacher Collins syndrome,' Christina echoed, and he could see her flipping through a mental medical textbook. Had she hit the right chapter? Craniofacial anomalies? Yep, she was getting to it. It sat there in an alphabetical list, somewhere below Moebius syndrome and Nager syndrome and Parry-Romberg syndrome.

He helped her out, just in case she'd turned to the wrong page. 'It's genetic. Rare. One in ten thousand births. If it's carried by either parent, it's a dominant gene, so any child they may have has a fifty-fifty chance of having it, which may have implications for Amber down the track if she wants to have kids.'

She listened intently, nodding every now and then, narrowing her eyes, never taking them from his face. He could see how much she wanted his words to solve something, get the two of them back on track towards a shared future, but he knew it wouldn't happen. She looked fragile suddenly, even though he knew how strong she was, and he wanted to hold her, feel that fabulous contrast between his bulk and her pliant grace.

'And, of course, it can be a spontaneous mutation,' he went on, struggling with the detail for a moment.

Was he hiding behind all this medical stuff?

Trying to scare her off with it?

Yes, definitely that.

'On chromosome five, if you want to get technical. And that's what it was in Amber's case. No one else in the family carries the gene.'

He paused for breath, but he was ready to keep going, to answer her questions. He was pretty sure he knew what she'd ask and he had his responses ready.

Yes, unfortunately in Amber it was severe. Yes, with the characteristic undeveloped external ears, down-slanting eyes, absent cheekbones and eye-socket floors, and small, slanting jaw. Yes, she'd needed numerous surgical procedures and she still faced more. She'd almost died at birth when her condition had taken the medical staff by surprise. She hadn't been able to breathe or feed normally.

Now Amber had a conductive hearing aid and a tracheostomy which was operative at night and capped during the day to give her a voice. A jaw distraction procedure was coming up, and after that they hoped she'd be able to lose the trach but didn't yet know for sure. She might get an internal hearing device some time in the next few years.

And she was a great, terrific, fabulous kid, fifteen years old now, bright and articulate and creative, comfortable with herself, but, yes, she got stared at sometimes, she got teased, she got asked insensitive questions, and he was so proud about how she handled it.

As for how his mother and stepfather handled it…well, he'd get to all that next.

But Christina didn't go in the expected direction at all. Instead, she jumped ahead so far and so fast that he was left open-mouthed with his head spinning. She put her knife and fork down on the plate on either side of her barely touched meal and pushed her chair back. Her ponytail swung like a horse flicking a fly, and her warm brown eyes were blazing.

And even while he was shocked by her reaction, he still had time to think how gorgeous and dynamic she looked.

'That?' she said angrily. 'Something like that…you haven't told me in two years… And you tell me now, as if it totally explains why we're at this impasse with each other? It doesn't explain anything, Joe! I've read about Treacher Collins. I'm a doctor.'

'So you know it can be pretty serious.'

'You're hiding your sister just because of her facial deformity, the way people used to hide the family lunatic and believe they could never marry because there was a streak of insanity in the family? I don't believe it! I don't understand why you haven't told me any of this in two years, and why you're telling it to me now as if it explains…!'

She stopped.

Started again a few seconds later.

'No. Actually, I do understand. And that makes it worse. A heck of a lot worse.'

Her voice broke and she rushed out of the kitchen, and he knew it was because she was too upset to stay. He could hear her gasping, angry sobs, and for a moment he was tempted to let her have it her way. Leave her alone, if she wanted to be left alone. Let her be angry with him, if that was what she believed about his motivations. It would define the end of their relationship more clearly.

But then he rebelled. He'd gone along with her ultimatum so far because he hadn't felt that he had the right to do anything else. If he wasn't promising a future for the two of them, then she had every reason to turf him over to the doctors' house, every right to put her own needs first and keep her options open.

This time, though...

He couldn't let her get it so wrong.

Rising from the table, he listened but couldn't work out where she'd gone. The house seemed too quiet. Then he heard the back screen door flap and followed her in that direction. Standing on the veranda, he saw her prowling the back garden, where a streetlamp shining through from the next street gave everything the bluish-white hue of moonlight.

He went down the steps and confronted her angry, wounded expression. 'Christina, it's more complicated than you think.'

'Listen to yourself say that! Whose fault is it?'

'Mine. I know that.'

'So change!'

He laughed tiredly.

Christina drawled, 'I know. You just said it. It's more complicated than I think.'

'The reason I didn't tell you is not because I was ashamed of Amber, if that's what you're thinking. Hell, no! I'm incredibly proud of her.' He outlined the surgical procedures she'd had, the struggles she still faced. 'And it wasn't because I thought you'd be horrified about her either. I know you're not like that.'

'Then why?'

He sighed, facing the unpleasant prospect of finding the right words, picking his way through. 'Amber's birth destroyed my mother's marriage to my stepfather,' he began.

'I thought they were still together.'

'They are, but it's only because neither of them trusts the other to do the right thing for Amber. My stepfather has a drinking problem. It was always there in the background, but it got worse after Amber was born. He makes an enemy of every doctor who treats her. He doesn't trust my mother to "stand up to them". And sometimes he's been right. There have been a couple of times when, in hindsight, the wrong decisions have been made—like when they tried to take out her trach at one point, and had to put it back in because she couldn't get enough air without it. New Zealand just doesn't have enough doctors with enough experience of this condition.'

'Your parents couldn't have taken her elsewhere for another opinion?'

'There isn't the money. I'm putting in a lot to support them as it is.'

'The New Zealand health system doesn't cover all the costs?'

'When you're talking about expensive, ongoing procedures like the ones Amber has had, and still needs, no health system covers all the costs. For a start, some of her surgery is regarded as cosmetic. Or elective, and subject to waiting lists, which mean the timing ends up all wrong. And some costs are impossible to quantify, like the fact that my mother can't hold down a decent job when Amber has needed so much of her time. I know my mother would like to leave my stepfather. She married him when she was still in pieces over my father's death, and she mistook his domineering for strength. She's stronger herself now, but she believes that staying with him is best for Amber. Because of the way he alienates doctors, because his priorities for Amber aren't always right, because of the money. She fights to maintain the partnership, even if it's just on the surface. She doesn't want to rock the boat.'

'And neither did you, with me. You just wanted the R&R. You didn't trust me enough to tell me any of this, because you thought that if you did, I might not stick around for the fun times you wanted from me. Do you know how much that hurts?'

'Would you really stick around, Tink? Would you really take it on? Every cent that I save by working over here goes to my parents for Amber. To my mother, really. If I can make enough of a nest-egg to convince her she can afford to leave my stepfather, then that's hers, too. Amber has such courage. I'm not going to let her down. She's only just turned fifteen. I'm staying in Auckland, probably permanently and definitely until Amber is grown up and independent. I'm not moving elsewhere because if I wasn't in Auckland, I think the family situation would blow sky-high. I don't trust my stepfather's intentions. I don't trust my mother's strength. I trust Amber absolutely, but she has enough on her plate just dealing with the surgery and the self-image. If I left…' He shook his head. 'Bad enough being here one week in four. If it wasn't for the money…'

'Money? I have money. My grandmother left me $60,000 as well as this house.'

He laughed. 'That would have gone down well. Christina sweetheart, I love you, give me your inheritance so I can spend it on my sister.'

'When people love each other—my God, Joe, you of all people should understand this—they take on each other's lives, each other's problems.'

To Joe's ears it sounded sweet, seductive…naïve. It sounded like a siren song whose hypnotic influence he had to fight or it would weaken him and drag him under.

'I don't want this,' he said. He tried not to sound harsh, but knew he had to sound firm. 'You don't know what you're offering. Christina, it doesn't work, that whole idea of a problem shared being a problem halved. Not when it's stuff like this.'

'So you're the only one who gets to be a hero. Boy, you have tickets on yourself, don't you?'

'It's not like that. Your involvement would only compound the pressure. And I've got enough pressure. That's exactly what I've loved about being here, being with you. So much less pressure.'

She paced around the garden some more, still angry and agitated. Her breathing came in little gasps and he knew it was because of the battle inside her between yelling and crying. In the end, she did both.

'Go! Just go, OK? If you're going to keep talking like this, I don't want to hear it. I never thought I could be this angry with you. I—I can't even talk about it any more.'

He looked at her and saw that she meant it. And she was right, of course. He'd said what he had to say, what she deserved to hear—the basic explanation. Now he needed to leave her alone to digest it, and to come around to his point of view.

Love wasn't enough, if what two people needed from each other was so totally different, and in such conflict. It wasn't enough if one of them was only going to drag the other one down. He should never have said the L word, because for her it meant a future, and for him it didn't.

He just didn't have the space.

Todd had driven to the gate to pick him up, as he'd promised to do.

Promise? It had been more like a threat.

'Take your days off, then, dag-face, but if you're not back on this spot by five o'clock Tuesday afternoon, I'm not waiting.'

Jack had dropped from the cab of the truck that had given him his last lift at four forty-five. His watch read six-ten as Todd's ute scrabbled to a halt in the dirt on the far side of the gate.

'Hungover?' was Todd's cheerful greeting. He'd wound his window down but hadn't bothered to get out of the car.

'Head's splitting,' Jack answered on a drawl.

Of course it wasn't true. He never wasted too much honesty on Todd. Digger wasn't so bad. The kind of bloke who respected you if you earned it. Todd didn't have enough discrimination to respect anyone.

'Come on, fathead, climb over,' he said.

'I want my back pay first.'

Todd laughed. 'What, you think I carry that kind of cash around with me?'

'I know you do.' He pointed at the back of the ute. 'It's taped to the side of the tyre well, right there.' In a plastic

packet, and the tape was that strong cloth kind. It was a pretty obvious hiding place.

Todd's eyes narrowed, but he recovered quickly. 'And where are you going to keep it?' he jeered.

'Lend me the tape and I'll find somewhere.' Against his own chest, probably.

'Half. You can have half. Gesture of good faith.'

Jack nodded. He hadn't expected more. To be honest, he hadn't known what he'd do, what his next move would be, if Todd called his bluff and refused to give him anything, but apparently the man needed him enough that he had some leverage now.

Gotta strategise a bit more in future, Jack, he told himself.

Todd was going to shift his stash, for a start, so Jack would need to learn the new hiding place as soon as he could, or the first half of his back pay might be all he'd ever get. And he should listen to his instincts and think a bit more about what was going on here. Why did Todd carry so much in cash anyhow? And those reports he came back with from 'the boss'—they were inconsistent sometimes.

The trip down south, even though Jack hadn't got where he wanted to go, seen who he wanted to see, had cleared his head, hardened his spirit. The night he'd spent, two days ago, dossed down on some damp shrubs behind the bus shelter at the hospital, he'd barely slept but he'd thought a lot, watching the patterns of bright and dark through the hospital windows.

It hadn't been a waste of time, as he'd thought at first. It had fortified him somehow, and when he'd set off again, walking north beside the highway just before dawn, he'd felt as if he was carrying something new and good inside him. Pining and mooning and dreaming didn't do you any good. You had to plan, and you had to take action.

She had seen something in him that no one else ever had. She'd told him he was strong and smart.

Time to start proving it.

On Wednesday, Christina had the day off.

She knew it would be tough. Sleeping in until nine-thirty had been a stupid strategy of denial. Now she just felt thick-headed and sluggish, only getting to breakfast at a quarter past ten. On top of it all, she felt nauseous, and two pieces of buttered toast with Vegemite didn't do enough to settle the feeling.

Yesterday, she and Glenn and Grace had done another clinic flight, one of their regular island hops. It was like a different world. Ocean instead of desert. Tourists irritated that illness had disrupted their expensive break, instead of locals trying to get on with their normal lives. The cases had all been pretty routine, no drama, no patients to bring in to the ED. She hadn't set eyes on Joe at all.

She'd arrived home before dark, but the empty house hadn't felt any better in daylight than it did at night. She'd co-opted a couple of people into going for a drink at the Black Cockatoo, but then she'd only had a single lemon squash and left after less than an hour. The smell of beer had made her feel ill, and the noise of the other drinkers had jarred.

She knew she'd have to advertise for a new occupant for Joe's empty room very soon, because she would fall into too many bad habits if she stayed on her own.

Not eating right, for example.

Those plates of congealed scrambled egg had just got

chucked in the bin on Monday night, and she'd had an evening meal of tea and chocolate biscuits instead.

She wouldn't look after herself unless she had someone here to shame her into it, she knew that. What she really needed was someone *she* could look after, someone to give her the incentive to have salad ingredients and vegetables, cheese and cold sandwich meat in the fridge, decent bread in the pantry, a bathroom she cleaned twice a week, someone she wouldn't want to appear in her pyjamas in front of at noon on a Saturday.

Megan Cooper.

Megan and her baby.

The idea came to her as if a voice had spoken it in her ear, and her brain was slow to catch up.

Could it work? Would Megan be interested?

She was almost ready for discharge. She was only still there because she hadn't got the feeding thing sorted out, and because the family situation was complicated. Jackson would need a little longer, and Megan would probably spend most of her time at the hospital by his side even once she was no longer officially a patient herself, but it would help her to have a place she could come to just to crash occasionally, do laundry, eat a home-cooked meal.

'I'm going to ask,' she decided, speaking out loud to her coffee-cup. It was a poor substitute for the conversation partner she really wanted in her kitchen right now.

Don't go down that path, Christina.

Stay practical.

What else did she need to consider?

Rent? She wouldn't charge anything. Or not until Megan was well and truly on her feet anyhow, and then only for the sake of the girl's pride.

Joe had insisted on paying for his room for the first few

months, two years ago, but it had been obvious that he had been trying to save every possible cent that he earned here. Christina had seized on a couple of leaky taps as an opportunity as soon as she'd realised.

'I'm hopeless at that stuff, Joe, and I'm not interested in learning. I'll call a plumber…or if you have the skills, could you do it? Could we make it in lieu of rent, that you'll tackle those jobs that come up from time to time?'

He'd agreed, and she hadn't had a leaky tap, a loose board on the veranda, a wayward lawn, a sticky door or a blown light bulb since.

Why did all her thought tracks come back to Joe?

She made a growling noise, put her coffee-cup on the draining-board and focused again.

Rent. The issue of rent. Megan might not be able to barter her rent with practical skills. She'd been raised on a farm, but she was young and not ready for motherhood and she had a fragile baby to take care of. But it would be great to have the two of them in the house. Especially great to have a baby…

Tick, tick, tick. Biological clock. No father in sight. *Christina Farrelly!*

It was all arranged about Megan and the baby by the end of the afternoon.

'And I've put a box in the staff tea-room, Christina,' Jill Shaw told her, in her office. 'For donations of clothing and personal items for Megan and Honey and the baby. Honey had nothing when she flew in with you.'

'That's right, only her handbag.'

'She's bought some underwear in town, but we all know that money is tight for that family so she doesn't want to invest in a whole new wardrobe.'

'That's thoughtful of you, Jill,' Christina said.

'Yes, well. Some kinds of needs are obvious and easy to meet.'

Charles appeared in the doorway, having done his usual magic trick with the silent wheelchair. He was pretty magic at catching up on a conversation halfway through, too. 'We're talking about the box for the Coopers?' he asked.

'Yes, Dr Wetherby, I hope you approve.'

'Don't approve of the Dr Wetherby bit, Jill,' he said with a grin, 'but the rest of it's fine. There are three packets of nappies in there already, I noticed.'

'Oh, wonderful!' Christina answered. 'We're going to have to empty it three times a day.'

'I thought of that. It's a big box,' Jill retorted.

And finally she smiled.

Christina caught Charles's lingering look of approval at the change in Jill's face, and wondered about it. First Brian clucking over their director of nursing, now Charles. Prickly Jill had been a little softer lately. She was getting over her bad marriage, and her divorce. What might happen next? Brian and Jill? And what about Charles? Had he ever thought of marriage?

She couldn't wonder about it for long, because Charles had something to tell her.

'I've spoken to Glenn. I'm hitching a ride with you tomorrow.'

'On the clinic run? Springing a performance evaluation on us?'

'Do you think you need one?'

'Not urgently!' She grinned, and got the same approving look that he'd given to Jill.

He cares about all of us, that's all it is, she decided. Cares about his hospital and his staff. Brian's free to give

Jill a shoulder to cry on, and my dinner with him tomorrow is nothing more than filling in time. There's no mess…

Except the one between her and Joe.

No one could help her with that.

'Well, you're safe from inspection for the moment anyhow. I'm taking a day off,' Charles said. He frowned suddenly. 'You and Glenn and Grace are heading into the Gulf country, but you're going to take a detour first and drop me at Wetherby Downs.'

CHAPTER SEVEN

'How did it go today, Christina?' Charles asked as they climbed into the air, away from Wetherby Downs.

For once, his mind didn't seem fully focused where his mouth was, Christina thought. He had asked the question absently, his gaze straying back to the arid view from the aircraft window before he'd even heard her answer.

'Pretty routine,' she told him through their headsets. The twin engines droned on. 'Although I took a few bloods and tissue samples. We might have some follow-up, bringing a couple of people in for treatment.'

'Mmm,' he answered, still looking at the ground below. 'Lord, it's dry! I could see it on the way out this morning, the perceptible shading off of the green into brown as soon as we were over the mountains.'

Christina looked at the land below. It spread out like a map, the detail of the terrain clear but flattened by their increasing altitude. She saw cattle moving toward a wide, tree-lined loop of creek, and a windmill turning lazily against the backdrop of dry, red earth.

'How is Wetherby Downs?' she asked

They'd picked Charles up from the private airstrip at the huge station fifteen minutes ago on their way back to Crocodile Creek. The strip was a couple of kilometres from the main homestead, whose location was marked from the air by its groupings of desert-hardy trees. He'd just been sitting there on his own, with his wheelchair parked by a fence-post as he'd watched the approach of the plane. For some reason no one had waited with him after dropping him off, and he'd looked like a very solitary figure.

Helpless, you would have said, if you hadn't known him the way they knew him in Crocodile Creek.

'It's on the market,' he answered bluntly, his jaw tight.

'That bad?'

Christina couldn't believe it. She knew that on such a vast acreage there should still be water. Gunya Creek was spring-fed and permanent. It never dried up. Even if Charles's younger brother had had to sell off some stock to ease the burden on resources, a place of this size had its surplus capital from the good years invested—protected—elsewhere.

'The cattle are doing fine,' Charles said. 'It was my decision to put the place up for sale, since I have partial ownership, and it has nothing to do with the drought. Everyone's going to know about it soon enough, so there's no point in secrecy.'

'Why?' she asked blankly. She could see that Grace and Glenn were both listening, just as curious.

'Because even with a direct approach from me, my brother refused to help the Coopers, not in their current crisis, and not by giving them back the creek access they had for three generations. And since my father neglected to specify in his will that the family property was not to be sold in order for one of the part-owners to realise their capital share, I'm doing just that—forcing the sale. There are pastoral companies who'll be very interested, because they know they can push for a rock-bottom price in this drought.'

'But, Charles—'

He ignored her. 'I spent some time sitting with Jim Cooper last night. We were pretty good mates in our teens. Now he's a broken man. If there's any chance of him getting back on his feet, physically and emotionally, he's going to need a miracle.'

'And you've found one?' Christina asked eagerly. Everyone at the hospital wanted the best possible outcome for the Cooper family.

Charles shook his head. 'I tried. But my brother is a pompous idiot, and weak with it, which doesn't leave me with a lot of choice. If Philip isn't going to honour his obligations as part of the local community, then I'm going to put my share of the money from the sale of Wetherby Downs towards helping the community in a different way. Wygera needs a swimming pool. Crocodile Creek needs better scanning equipment. The doctors' house could do with a new fridge, I'm told. Any suggestions to add to the shopping list are very welcome.'

Well, he'd shocked all of them!

'Th-that's very generous of you, Charles,' Christina told him.

'It isn't,' he snapped back tersely. 'It's blackmail. I've used two strategies on Philip over the course of our lives. I've protected him, and I've ignored him. Both of those strategies appear to have failed. We'll see what happens with this one.'

'Is this…?' Grace began, sounding unusually tentative. 'Charles, you've told us this isn't a secret, but—'

'But does that mean I want the news spreading like wildfire? Of course I don't, but it'll happen anyway. Tell whoever you like.'

Had anyone ever seen Charles like this before?

Christina certainly hadn't. She wondered what had gone on between the two men, and whether Charles's lonely wait for the aircraft was significant. Who had driven him out to the airstrip? Why hadn't they stayed? Who had been the angriest, Philip or Charles?

Nobody felt much like talking after this, and she was glad to realise that the flight back to Crocodile Creek would soon be over.

Famous last words. They got a radio call to divert to Wygera on the way in, to pick up a patient. The rescue helicopter was transferring a young woman in pre-term labour at twenty-eight weeks gestation down south to a hospital with a high-level neonatal unit, and couldn't be spared for an emergency at the settlement right now.

Wygera.

Joe had gone out there with a nurse on a clinic visit today, Christina knew, and her body went into fight-or-flight mode when she thought about seeing him. That queasy feeling from yesterday was back, and flying through a patch of rough air didn't help.

She and Joe hadn't parted well on Monday night. She'd looked up Treacher Collins syndrome on the internet the previous day, but all that had done had been to strengthen her belief that if Joe really cared about her, he should let her fully into his life. He was so proud of his half-sister. Christina would have loved to meet her, but clearly Joe never planned to let that happen.

She had been angry, hurting about it, questioning Monday's decisions and reactions, ever since.

But no lightning bolts of clarity had hit. Was she right to feel angry? Was she crazy to keep on looking for ways to give him another chance? What could she do to prove that he was wrong?

Joe and nurse Lindsay Palmer met them beside the airstrip, in the staff vehicle they'd used to drive there from

Crocodile Creek that morning. In the back of the vehicle, stretched awkwardly along the back seat, they had a kid with his arm curled protectively around some rickety thing that looked like a school craft project.

'Appendicitis,' Joe reported, yelling over the slowly subsiding propeller noise. He flashed Christina a glance and they both forgot to smile or say hello, too distracted by how complex their feelings were.

Lindsay gave everyone a brief greeting.

'Not sure how much detail you got on the radio,' Joe continued. His habitual good cheer seemed forced today, which was no surprise. 'I'm hijacking the plane because I think he's ruptured already, and we still have patients to see. Not to mention a thirty-mile drive back being less than ideal for young Shane.'

'How bad is he?' Christina asked.

'Not as bad as you'd think. Pain-wise, that is. He had the characteristic protective walk when his mother brought him in—he didn't want to come, still doesn't. Very tender when I got him lying flat and had a feel, but the tenderness was atypical. Mildly febrile. No nausea, although his mother said he had some last night. No vomiting, though. Then when I was debating what we should do with him, he started telling us something had popped and it wasn't hurting nearly so much any more and could he keep on with his model now, please?'

'His model?' Grace queried.

'The thing he's holding. It's a design for the new swimming pool and it's got some terrific ideas, actually. I said he could bring it with him, since he wasn't one bit keen to come without it.' He stepped closer to the plane and raised his voice. 'Charles, could we swap jobs for the rest of today?'

'Me take over the clinic with Lindsay?' Charles called back. 'Makes sense. I'd like to spend a bit of time out here. They've been through such a lot lately.'

They all knew that with his wheelchair he couldn't do anything useful, medically, in the confined space of the plane, and that having Joe back at the hospital could be vital if resources were stretched thin by any other emergency. Cal would operate.

'Glenn?' Charles said.

'Yep.' The pilot knew what to do. He had soon jumped down to the hard-baked clay of the strip to unfold Charles's wheelchair for the short transfer to the vehicle. Charles's upper-body strength and agility made the shift from chair to front passenger seat smooth and fast, and the wheelchair was re-folded and put in the back, along with some equipment they hadn't needed that day.

'Am I going in the plane?' Shane asked.

He looked about ten. Straw for hair, sleeveless flannel shirt, big eyes like glossy buttons. He could have obtained gainful employment as a scarecrow, he was obviously a handful, and you liked him as soon as you looked at him.

'Yes, you're going in the plane and, yes, you can bring your model,' Joe told him.

'It's the best one,' Shane said. 'Did you see Roddie's? It wasn't as good, but he says he's making it better. Everyone's working on 'em now. It was my idea!' He sounded affronted.

'We'll have a competition,' Charles announced with dour satisfaction from the passenger seat of the car, his face still as grim as it had been since they'd picked him up. 'It's perfect. All the kids at Wygera, anyone who wants to enter. This pool is not just going to be a big cement bathtub surrounded by dirt. It's going to be properly landscaped, really attractive, almost a water park, if we can manage it. It would be great to get the kids' ideas. The prize for the best model is... Dammit, what's the bloody prize? Fast-food vouchers? It's got to be something better than that. I'll have a think. Lindsay?'

'The prize?' The older nurse looked startled and a little blank. She didn't know that her hospital administrator had decided to force the sale of his family heritage that afternoon. Grace looked as if she was tempted to give over the goss right now.

But of course there wasn't time.

'No, I mean, let's drive, finish that clinic,' Charles answered the other nurse.

'Shane, up you go,' Joe was saying. 'Your mum's coming in the car with Dr Wetherby when he's finished at the clinic. She wants to pack an overnight bag for you first.'

Back in the plane, as Lindsay and Charles drove off, Christina was already getting out the IV equipment. They would need to hit him with a barrage of antibiotics, and they wouldn't wait for confirmation that the appendix had indeed blown. Shane looked uncomfortable, in more pain than he was letting on, but still consumed with the issue of the pool design.

'If there's a competition, there should be a prize for whose idea it was to make models, as well as for the best one,' he said. 'Tell that other doctor. The weather one.'

'Dr Wetherby? We will,' Christina answered. 'But not right now.'

'He's selling, Joe,' Grace came in. 'He told us today. He's using his part-ownership to force through the sale of Wetherby Downs.'

Joe whistled.

'Yes,' Grace agreed. 'I'm pretty shocked.'

Christina didn't join in. She thought Grace was probably attempting to take the heat, distract Joe and herself from each other.

Thanks, Grace. Yes, it's tough, being shut up in a plane with Joe. You're right, I want to cry or yell, so if you can keep the conversation ball bouncing, I'm grateful. And, yes, you'd probably also like to hear, at some point, what he and I talked about on Monday night, and how angry I got.

She hadn't found the right opportunity for that conversation with Grace yet. Probably could have if it had felt easier to open her mouth on the subject. But it felt…hard. Her stomach sank with reluctance every time she thought about it.

She swabbed a patch of skin on the inside of Shane's elbow with antiseptic, coaxed a vein into greater prominence and slipped the needle in. Shane didn't flinch. He was still clutching his model, which was made out of plastic margarine containers and cereal packet cardboard and silver and gold cigarette pack paper and half a dozen other makeshift things.

'See, it has to have water jets, and a couple of slides…'

'This tube is going to stay in for a while, Shane, so I'm going to tape it in place, OK?' she cut in.

'And a wading pool for the little kids, and a deep bit for the slide to go into…'

Glenn began his preparations for taxi and take-off.

'And it has to have grass, and shade, and look like… like…you know, you *have* to go there, you can't stay away. What're those places? Oh-ay-sisses.'

'An oasis?'

'Yes. Has to be like one of those.'

'It sounds great, Shane.'

'I'll be bringing togs and towel out to Wygera myself,' Joe agreed. 'Should see the splash when I do a bomb into the water. People scatter. OK, now we're giving you some medication, Shane. But that's going through the IV so you don't need to worry about a bad taste in your mouth.'

'Speaking of which,' Grace came in, 'if it's hurting, I can give you a squirt of this stuff, Shane. It tastes OK, you've probably had it before.'

The flight was uneventful, including a textbook-smooth landing and no smiles from Glenn.

'He's a good kid,' Joe commented to Christina as the noise level in the aircraft subsided and they taxied towards the ambulance waiting beside the tarmac.

Shane was lying quietly, probably still thinking about his model. The double transfer from plane to ambulance to hospital when an emergency admission came by fixed wing aircraft wasn't ideal. The helipad was better placed, directly adjacent to the hospital, even though the cost had been higher to have it that way.

'Good patient, too,' Joe added.

'I like the model,' Christina said.

'Wouldn't want to contemplate the budget for it.'

'Charles seems very determined that it won't be an issue.'

'Do you think he'll really force the sale?' Joe looked sceptical.

'Well, he said himself, after we'd picked him up from Wetherby Downs, that it was blackmail.' Instinctively, because she was talking about something so sensitive, she leaned closer, and both she and Joe noticed, felt the familiar intimacy.

His dark gaze flicked down to her arm close to his, and lifted again, moving over her body almost like a caress. The very air between them felt different. Her skin felt different. The way her lungs filled.

She took a careful breath and continued, 'But even if the sale doesn't go through, I've had the impression that Wetherby resources could find enough capital for a community swimming pool without liquidising their major asset.'

Joe dropped his voice. Had he been listening to what she'd just said? She didn't think so. 'Are you going to the party at the doctors' house tonight?' His jaw jutted, making him look strong and stubborn.

Party? No, she was going out to dinner with Brian. But she didn't want to tell Joe about that because it sounded like a transparent piece of rebound dating.

Which it wasn't. She wasn't remotely ready for rebound dating yet.

'Party?' she echoed.

'Dora Grubb's birthday, spur-of-the-moment idea of Cal's.' Dora and her husband Walter were stalwarts on the house-keeping side of hospital activity. 'She's been a treasure lately, taking care of Gina and Cal's young CJ, and they thought Georgie could do with a nice night, too, after dealing with her mother's death. I think you should come, Tink.'

'Why?'

He didn't have an answer. Probably because her question had been sharp and angry and pointless.

'I'm sorry, Joe,' she said.

'Because you're not going to come?'

She closed her eyes. 'Because I snapped at you. I'm not angry with you about...' She waved a hand. 'Party invitations.'

'But you are angry. Still.'

'Yes.'

'We'll talk about it tonight.'

'Sheesh, Joe! Two years we don't talk about anything important—'

'No?' He looked startled.

'No! But suddenly this week talking is the magic bullet?'

'I think we talked about a lot of things that were important,' he said quietly.

She ignored him. 'We talked on Monday—'

'You know, talking about mowing the lawn can be important if there's the right spirit behind it. Saying, please, pass the milk, or did you see that goal in the last minute of the game? Talking isn't everything. It's the actions behind the talk that count. The spirit behind it.'

Christina was in no mood to listen to this kind of philosophy. 'And we ended up angrier!' she finished.

'You're snapping again, Tink.'

'Well, this time there's no apology!'

But there was a safety in feeling able to show her anger that she didn't fully understand or appreciate until she was out with Brian that night. She'd gone straight home after the flight and hadn't heard an update on young Shane, so she was happy when Brian could give her one.

'The appendix was ruptured, as Joe thought,' he said over dinner. 'It was tucked behind the bowel so Cal couldn't get it out via laparoscopy. He had to go in through an old-fashioned incision, but he didn't muck around in there and the boy will be fine once the infection's brought under control.'

'That's good to hear, Brian.'

Christina was a lot less happy about the ambient backdrop to the update.

Brian had brought her to Mike Poulos's parents' very swishy three-star restaurant, which was part of the Athina hotel.

Low-key, she wanted to protest. You promised me it would be low-key. Pizza or burgers. And that was the only reason I said yes.

With its glorious ocean views, wall-sized aquarium of tropical fish, imported chef and prices to match, the Athina's restaurant was not low-key!

And Brian didn't pretend to think it was either. He had

arrived at her door earlier with a dozen roses, and had persuaded her to change into 'something dressier' before he would head out. She'd abandoned her denim skirt and cotton shirt and put on a pair of elegant black trousers and a shimmery top in rich metallic colours that fell from thin straps to drape across her front and left her shoulders bare. She'd even put her hair up with pins.

This time she fitted the bill…which was going to be huge. Brian had called ahead to the restaurant to order some special lobster dish for two that wasn't on the menu, he'd chosen one of the most expensive Chardonnays on the wine list and he kept requesting love songs from the live musician.

Christina was furious.

But how could she say so?

It was just conceivable that you could yell at a man for treating you like a cheap date, but to yell at him for the opposite reason? Because he was lavishing a two-hundred-dollar dinner and large quantities of special attention on her when he'd insisted this was just between friends?

She would have yelled if it had been Joe.

Light-bulb moment.

She was comfortable with Joe. They were safe enough with each other to get angry. Couldn't he see how important that was?

But she couldn't yell at Brian.

And couldn't *he* see how wrong this whole evening was?

'I've always thought you were pretty special, Christina,' he told her.

No, no, no! I haven't been sending out those kind of signals!

'Well, you know,' she joked deliberately, 'I did my medical degree at Sydney University and my professors were pretty happy with me.'

'That's not what I mean, and you know it.'

Yes, darn it, I do know it, but take the hint!

He didn't.

'I know it's too soon—'

'It takes time, doesn't it? I think Jill's only just getting over her divorce. She's a terrific woman, Brian. I hadn't seen it until recently, and I think she really values your support,' she gabbled desperately.

'And, of course, I'm happy to give it, but Jill is not who I want to talk about right now. Tell me more about the real Christina Farrelly. Is she the fabulous woman I think she is?'

No, she's a complete hag, with a definite depletion of brain cells this week, Christina thought, and she should never have come out with Brian.

'She's pretty tired,' Christina said truthfully. She didn't want to hurt him. Where was the human compassion in doing that? Not to mention the career advantage.

By skipping dessert and gulping her wine, she brought the evening to an earlier finish than she'd been afraid of. Brian looked at his watch. 'I'll run you home, but let's call in at the hospital first. I have a couple of errands to take care of.'

He wanted to show off the fact that they'd been out, she soon realised.

Not to Joe.

After some embarrassing encounters with people like Cal and Georgie, which Christina was sure Brian had engineered in order to parade their date, meeting up with Joe was the one chance event of the evening, and she was so relieved to see him that she couldn't help letting it show.

Joe Barrett, I'd a hundred times rather spend an angry evening with you than a smoochy evening with Brian. Can I tell you that? Does it mean something? Will it help? Can you save me from Brian right now?

'Joe?' She grabbed his arm and steered him down the corridor towards the surgical ward, while trying to make it look as if he was steering her. 'Give me an update. You're looking in on Shane?'

'Just have. His mother's with him and he's doing pretty well. Pretty groggy from the PCA.' The abbreviation stood for patient-controlled anaesthesia. 'He's pressing the button for it a lot.'

'What's he having? Morphine?'

'Yes. He's still on oxygen, fluids, anti-emetic, antibiotics. Cal did a good job as usual. Didn't have him in Theatre too long.'

'Routine, then.'

'So far. And we're getting bowel sounds. Which means he should be back to working on his swimming-pool design in a few days.'

'I hope Charles goes ahead with his competition idea.'

'Have you ever known Charles not to go ahead with any of his ideas? Eh, Brian?'

He smiled dutifully, while Christina laughed.

'Good point,' she said. 'I'd like to see Shane myself. Do you mind coming back with me, Joe? Now?'

Please?

She turned the minimal acceptable number of degrees back in Brian's direction. 'Brian, thanks for a really lovely meal. Don't worry about getting me home. I'll thumb a lift with someone.'

He frowned. 'Christina, that's dangerous.'

She hadn't meant it literally. 'I'll make sure it's someone whose last name I already know,' she told him patiently, and didn't wait for his reaction.

Still dragging Joe with her, she took a couple more determined steps in the direction of the ward, and Joe murmured, 'I like this arm-clutching exercise. New anger-management technique?'

'Oh, Joe…!' It was almost a sob.

'Hey…Tink!'

'Don't make me laugh when I'm feeling like this.'

Brian had gone, finding some discretion at last. Joe and Christina both slowed and stopped.

'Forcible laughter induction procedure against the patient's will,' Joe teased, his voice only for her. The rest of the universe seemed to disappear. 'Grounds for a medical malpractice suit, I'd reckon.'

'Stop!' She pressed her hands to the sides of her head.

'Listen…' His voice dropped even lower. 'If I can get you to stop feeling angry, I'll do it, using fair means or foul. I never wanted us to get to this point.' He traced a soft line across her hand with his finger.

She gave a helpless sigh. 'You know what I've started to think? Being angry isn't such a bad thing, especially if we're talking about it. At least it means we have something real!' She reached out and brushed her knuckles against his forearm, loving its strength, no longer willing to surrender her right to touch him.

'Do we still have something at all, Tink?' His dark eyes wandered over her, and they stood even closer, enough to feel each other's heat. 'I thought we didn't.'

'Oh, we have something.' Her hand hovered over his shoulder, then dropped away again. If she touched his neck, he'd bend and kiss her. She knew he would, and that would be too hard to deal with.

'Great big wounds, if nothing else,' he suggested.

'Yeah? You have them, too?'

'You really think I'm breezing through the week? Living it up at the doctors' house? Cruising for chicks at the Black Cockatoo?'

If you feel the same way I do, why are we in this mess?
she wanted to yell at him. *Why are we putting ourselves
through this for no reason?*

Bloody heroes!

'Shall we just…go to the party, Joe?' she suggested,
knowing they couldn't get into an intense and personal conversation now, pull their lives apart and put them back together again just metres from patients in their beds.

'Yeah, let's,' he agreed.

So they went, walking in silence out of the hospital and
across the memorial garden in the soft night, not touching,
no longer a partnership, but still with so much going on.

And it was noted by numerous pairs of eyes that they
arrived together, even though they moved apart as soon as
separate groups of friends greeted them.

'So?' Grace demanded, cornering Christina in the big
kitchen a short while later. 'You look great. Brian took you
to the Athina, didn't he?'

'Yes, but that wasn't—'

'No, I know, it was a much bigger evening than you
wanted, but don't tell me about dinner with Brian. Tell me
about Joe. I saw you coming across the garden with him.'

Someone had turned the music up loud. A couple of kids
were dancing on the lawn, up past their bedtime. There
were people in the pool, and Gina was acting as a self-
appointed lifeguard. Joe was mooching around out there
as well. Brian put in an appearance, but didn't stay long.
Mrs Grubb had ignored her role as guest of honour and was
taking charge of the food.

Joe. Grace wanted to hear about Joe, the way she had
three days ago by the water-tank in Gunyamurra.

'Bottom line, Grace, it's the swan-wife issues,' Christina
told her friend.

'Oh, it is?' Grace looked intrigued. And worried.

'Yep. I was right. You were right. Sticks out a mile. In-credible that no one else in town has noticed the tell-tale dropping of flight feathers.'

'But seriously!' Grace yelled above the music.

'Seriously? OK. Swan-sister issues. Family issues.' She couldn't go into details. Joe had made it clear he didn't want it all talked about. 'A family he can't leave or let down,' was all she could say.

'And that you can't be a part of?'

'According to him. He's a go-it-alone kind of man, shouldering the whole lot, with a great big suffering hero complex, Grace.'

'Which only makes you love him more, even when you don't want to, because in our line of work you come across too many men who don't shoulder their responsibilities at all.'

Yes. Exactly.

'Why does it work that way, damn it?' Christina yelled back, over an extra-loud patch in the music. 'Love him, and get angry with him, and realise that I'm not doing myself any favours with any of it.'

Grace looked at her, tilted her head to one side and frowned. 'You know what? I'm starting to think there's a better way to look at this. I think the grieving period was premature.'

'OK, what's this now?' Christina let out a weary laugh. 'You're telling me the sky isn't falling after all? Is that what you're suddenly saying? It's not what you were saying on Monday at Gunyamurra, Grace O'Riordan.'

'Give him another chance.'

'Wha-a-at?'

'Didn't you say to me that if you knew why then you thought you could deal with it? Now you know why. The swan sister. Which is way better than the swan wife. So deal with it for a while, and see how that feels.'

'Have him back in his old room? It's all settled that Megan and the baby are going to move in.'

'Good. Because you don't want him back in his old room. He can stay in his new room, here. You want to give yourself some protection.'

'The protection of the two of us maintaining separate dwellings three kilometres apart, while I open up my heart and tell him, Here, rip into it.'

'See? You understand the situation perfectly.'

'Grace!'

'Christina, Christina. We all care about you, and you're a mess. If Joe had frolicked off into the sunset without a backward glance, like a certain recent pair of doctors I could mention, I'd want you to stick to your guns on this. Well, you'd have no choice. But look at him—'

'He's—?' Christina whirled around in search of him. She hadn't realised he was anywhere near. He'd been outside ten minutes ago. She found part of an arm and shoulder, the top of his head and one hip. Her view of him kept getting obscured by other people, but she went on looking in that direction anyway.

'Yep,' Grace said, looking the same way. 'Sticking his head in the drinks fridge, wearing a thousand-yard stare. Been doing it for the past five minutes. Doesn't have a clue what he's looking for. The thing's on its last legs anyhow, and with the influx of warm air he's generating, I'm not holding my breath for the beer and orange juice staying cold next week. You see, he's just as much of a mess as you are.'

'Which, according to you, is a good thing.'

'Has to be, doesn't it?' Grace answered gently. She looked at Christina for a moment. 'Think about it.'

Joe didn't give her a chance to do that. He emerged
drinkless from the fridge and caught sight of her. 'This is
where you've got to?' he said, as if he'd found her under
the front seat of the car, like a lost CD.

'I'm prepared to consider other locations to park myself.'

He didn't say another word, just grabbed her hand, en-
gulfing it like a big leather glove.

'Where are we going, Joe?'

'Beach? I don't know.'

'The beach sounds good. Will anyone…?'

'No. No one will care. They might notice, but they won't
care.'

There was no moonlight tonight, but the frilly white
edges of the waves seemed to throw off their own lumines-
cent glow. The sand felt cool and spongy. Joe stopped to
lever off his running shoes and roll his trousers to the knees.
He could never bear to have anything between his feet and
the beach. Christina kicked her shoes off, too, and they
walked the length of the cove to the rocky outcrop at the
foot of the bluff and found a flat, cool place to sit and talk.

'I'm glad I told you about Amber on Monday night,' Joe
said. 'I didn't think it would feel good afterwards, but it did.'

'Why didn't you think it would feel good?'

'Because I was getting my nice, separate universes all
mixed up.' He reached out for her hand again, didn't add
anything to his answer.

Christina thought about pushing. Why? Why did you
want separate universes in the first place? Why won't you
trust me or…or celebrate…when I say I want to be part of
any universe that you're in, forever, for the rest of our lives?

But then she remembered what he'd said about talking,
just that afternoon. She hadn't been in the right mood to
listen at the time, but the words had stayed in her mind all

the same. How you could talk about trivial, impersonal things like garden chores and TV sport and it could still mean something if there was the right spirit underneath. How actions said just as much as words. Or said more.

Meanwhile, his hand was talking to her. He had the back of it resting against the rock, his knuckles taking the roughness of the salt-crusted stone while her hand got to rest in the soft, warm bed of his big palm. The ball of his thumb slid back and forth across her skin, painting loose circles of sensation.

She looked down. Only this one point of contact. Two hands. One that was on the thin side, with a scattering of freckles and a current unmet need for moisturiser. The other built like a bear's paw, only smooth and brown. She couldn't see it, but she knew there was an old scar cutting across the pad of muscle below his thumb. Letting her gaze track upwards, she found the blue-black tattoo like a narrow bracelet on his upper arm, circling the strong muscle.

'I'm glad you told me about Amber, too,' she said at last. 'I only wish you'd done it sooner.'

'Don't go telling everyone in Crocodile Creek, will you?'

'Of course I won't!'

'She hates to think that people talk about her, even if she knows they mean well. She doesn't even like to hear me telling her too often that I'm proud of her.'

'How does she handle your parents and all their conflict?'

'I don't think she's quite realised yet that it should be different, that not all fathers are aggressive and loud and bullying, and secretly ready to put their daughters through any amount of plastic surgery necessary to make her look normal.'

'He wants that? For her to look normal?'

'No matter what the cost.' He picked up his previous

thread. 'And meanwhile that not all mothers are driven to living their most important emotions in secret, because Mum *knows* Amber only wants the surgery that's necessary for her health—heaven knows, that's extensive enough. She knows Amber doesn't want procedure after procedure in a doomed quest for the perfect supermodel eyes and nose, but she pretends to go along with Geoff, my stepfather. She sacrifices too much, tears herself in half agreeing with everyone, while Geoff rants and raves and drinks up half of what she tries to save.'

He shook his head. They'd both got tangled in what they were saying, in danger of losing the original thread. It happened when something was this complicated, emotionally.

'But you're offering Amber a different model of male behaviour,' Christina said. 'That's so good, Joe.'

'I'm just her brother.'

'She must think that brothers are pretty OK, then.'

'Hope so.'

More silence.

He eased his hand from the rock. She turned it over and traced the red indentations imprinted by the rough texture of the stone. 'Looks sore,' she said, thinking about Grace's advice to give him another chance.

'It's OK,' Joe said.

'Bloody hero!'

He grinned. 'Yeah, I'm a real nuisance.'

'You are!' She grinned back. Then she sighed.

His black eyes glimmered at her, steady and open.

Heroes had their good points.

She made her decision.

'Could I, please, kiss you, Joe?' she whispered.

CHAPTER EIGHT

'ARE you sure that's a good idea, Tink?' Joe said, even though the words felt as if they might kill him. 'Kissing me?'

'It's a brilliant idea.' She leaned in and touched the pads of her fingers to his lips. She wasn't grinning any more.

Neither was he. Her kiss felt as if it might kill him, too. He knew he shouldn't let it happen, but right now he didn't have it in him to say no when she was insisting yes. He just waited for her mouth.

It felt cool. It felt soft. She teased him, only brushing her lips against his, pressing them briefly then brushing them away. She took his face between soft hands and angled her head to one side, brushed his mouth again, angled her head the opposite way, dabbed a tiny bit of moisture with the tip of her tongue, just where his lips parted.

Then she sat back and pulled the pins out of her piled hair, combed the loosened strands with her fingers and shook them down around her shoulders, releasing a cloud of sweet, nutty scent into the air.

His groin tightened in a rush of heat. He wanted to grab her, ravish her, show her his strength, give in to his impatience as fast as a man could, and yet he held back. He'd been wanting this all week, thinking about it, remember-ing Sunday night and aching with loss and sheer physical frustration at the thought that it might never happen again.

Now she was offering, sweet and wicked at the same time, getting to the point as slowly, slowly as she could get away with, while his body responded lightning fast. He hid the speed and power of his reaction, still at a loss. He'd lis-tened to what she'd said she wanted on Sunday night, and had respected her right to make that decision. Now she was saying something different—backing down, really, saying that she'd decided it could work on his terms after all.

So what was his problem?

Christina didn't know either.

'Hey!' she whispered at last, letting her breath and the light touch of her fingernails caress his ear. 'It takes two.' She kissed a trail of sensation down his neck, threaded her fingers into his hair. His spine began to tingle.

'Yeah?' he growled. His body echoed the sceptical word with an unequivocal imperative of its own.

She's saying yes, idiot, so let's make it yes. Now!

'This is what you want?' he growled. She shrieked with surprised satisfaction as he engulfed her with his arms and half rolled, half carried her from the rocks onto the sand. 'Yes?' he growled again, as they rolled. He also meant, 'Here?'

And she knew it. 'Yes,' she told him, getting breathless.

She ended up on top and he pulled her close. She lay with her head pillowed on his chest and he stroked her silky hair, giving her one last chance to change her mind. She didn't speak. Then, with his eyes closed yet still able to find her unerringly, he cupped his palm against her jaw and turned her face towards his.

No games now. Their kiss turned deep and hungry at

once. They invaded each other's mouths, pushed at each other's clothing. Their bodies were shaking and they ignored the sand. And if anyone else decided to take a walk on this beach tonight… Well, this would be over pretty soon, the way they were each pulling the other towards the brink.

She sat up, sliding up his body to straddle his chest, and he opened his eyes, wanting to see her—see the hair that fell loosely over him, the lost, blissful expression on her face, the hunger and the beauty. And it was all there.

He watched as he touched her, running his hands along the fabric-covered thighs that squeezed against his chest, loving everything about her while still knowing that this wasn't enough. Or maybe it was the whole problem. He cared about her well-being too much to rope her into the complexity of his life.

She pulled her shimmery top over her head, her raised arms lifting and rounding her breasts in their dark lace bra. He reached up for her, running his hands over those jutting forms and then down the satin of her bare skin. During all of this, her eyes stayed closed, which meant he could keep watching her.

Watching her emotional nakedness, and her trust.

Watching just how much she gave to him, now as always.

And that was when he knew that they had to stop.

His hands stilled, resting on her hips. She waited, a little frown on her forehead. She was almost smiling, anticipating, waiting for him to cup her breasts again, or pull her down so he could reach the fastening of her bra. She thought he was teasing her.

'Joe…?'

He spoke the first part of his thought out loud. 'This feels so good.'

'So why are you making us wait?'

There was a beat of silence before he answered, 'Because we can't do this.' And even while he was saying it he was mentally kicking himself for abusing his body—and hers—with this much denial.

Ah, hell, saying it wasn't enough, he realised. He had to make a move.

He did so with an immense effort, lifting her off him, coaxing her sideways onto the sand, pulling himself up to sit so that he could protect his throbbing groin. His breathing came with an effort. She was looking at him, stricken and bewildered.

'Bit gob-smacked,' she said, making light of it. 'Thought it was going pretty well.'

'But what's changed, Tink?' he burst out. 'What's changed for you since I moved into the doctors' house three days ago that makes this suddenly OK now? Because you know about Amber? Because I said I was glad that you did?'

'Thought it was a pretty good start,' she answered lightly.

He wasn't fooled.

He knew the way her thinking had travelled. She thought they were going to do this in stages. Step one, Joe talks about his family and discovers it doesn't feel as difficult and bad as he might have thought. Step two, Christina comes to New Zealand for a holiday, meets Amber and their mother and Amber's Dad and tells Joe how great Amber is, and that there's hidden strength in his mother, and even a couple of qualities in his stepfather that she can connect with and admire. Step three, she throws herself into the whole situation with a hundred per cent of her heart and Joe feels so pressured by what she's prepared to sacrifice for his sake that he forgets how to breathe.

Which means, step four, they both suffocate.

He'd seen his mother stretching herself in ten directions at once, trying to fill the bottomless well of other people's needs. She'd come close to destroying herself in the process. And it wasn't that he thought men were stronger. But he thought that they often protected themselves better. They had a streak of selfishness that meant they would always look out for number one.

He'd done it himself with Christina. He'd known from the beginning that he couldn't stretch himself far enough to give her the whole package, so he hadn't tried. He'd protected himself, by keeping their relationship light and fun and restricted to the present. And he'd thought he'd been making the boundaries clear to her all along, but that hadn't helped.

Christina wouldn't protect herself at all. She didn't want to. She wanted to jump in with both feet. She was such a giving kind of person, but he couldn't let her do it, not when he'd seen just how badly wrong it could go.

'It's a mistake,' he said bluntly. 'This isn't going to work for either of us, because it isn't what you want, and you know it. You were right on Sunday night about ending it. Now you're talking about a "pretty good start" to a rekindling, as if I'm a fish on a line and you're carefully, carefully reeling me in.'

Although they weren't touching, he felt her stiffen in anger and shock. 'That's an awful—'

'No! I don't mean it the way it sounded,' he said quickly.

'That I'm a cold-blooded manipulator and you have a—a—*fish brain?* I hope not!' Her eyes flashed at him, because she had spirit as well as kindness.

'I mean, you're hoping for more,' he said. 'You're thinking that I've—*we've*—taken one step forward, so in a couple of months we'll take another.'

'Would that be terrible?' Her tone was mild but he knew she was still angry.

'There's only one place we can end up if we keep taking those steps,' he told her, 'and it's not somewhere I want to go.'

'Where do you want to go, Joe?' By this time she was close to tears, but she didn't want it to show, he could tell. Her voice sounded unnaturally hard as she asked the question.

'Nowhere,' he answered. 'Home. That's where I want to go right now.' He stood up. 'To the doctors' house.'

Where the sheets on his bed still smelled like her laundry detergent, and the flowers she'd put in a vase on the desk were beginning to wilt.

Sand showered out of Christina's top when she'd put it back on. It tickled on her skin and ended up in her trousers. She followed Joe up to the house. He took rapid strides, clearly as angry and frustrated as she was, getting well ahead of her in seconds. But every time he realised that she'd fallen behind he would stop and wait for her, which made her feel even angrier.

You're not my white knight. Stop acting like one.

Her feet dragged in the soft sand at the top of the beach. She felt drained and exhausted, queasy with it by this point. She didn't want to go back inside, where the party was still going on, although there were fewer cars parked out front now. Someone turned the music down lower as she and Joe approached. There were probably people trying to sleep by this time. It was after eleven, and most staff had to work tomorrow.

'I'm going to head off home, Joe,' she said.

He nodded carefully. 'How're you getting there? Brian picked you up, didn't he?'

She'd almost forgotten. 'I'll walk.'

'Not at this time of night.' The white knight was back, his armour shiny and well oiled. 'Let me duck inside and see if I can borrow someone's car to run you across.'

'Don't. Grace's car is still here. I'll ask if she can give me a lift. I can hang around for a bit if she's not ready to go. And you can go to bed, if you want, because you're not my personal host here tonight.'

He looked at her without speaking, then kind of apologised for both of them. 'I guess we're both tired.'

'Think so.' She tried to say it lightly, and ignored the way her body reacted just to the sight of him—weak knees, unsteady breathing, the works.

Looking as if it was an effort to get his feet moving, Joe went directly to his room via the veranda, and Christina went inside. She soon found Grace, who was laughing loudly in a group of four. But she was happy to leave right then, she said when Christina asked for a lift.

They talked in the car.

'So…Joe's not coming?' Grace asked. 'You know, bit of late-night fence-mending, nudge, nudge.'

Christina raked her teeth across her lower lip and sighed. 'I think it was the wrong advice, Grace.'

'Oh, hell, was it?' She looked stricken, the habitual twinkle of mischief gone from her blue eyes. 'How could it be wrong? You saw him stuck in front of the fridge like a thirsty ghost. Emily says he's been like that all week, a total mess. I'm really sorry. I should keep my nose out of my friends' business, shouldn't I?'

'It was what I wanted to hear, Grace, to be honest, but he went all noble and determined to save me from myself kind of thing, and I'm…' She stopped. 'Angry?' she tried, but it didn't feel right.

Well, nothing felt right.

'No, just numb,' she corrected.

'How about if I stay over? I can sleep on the couch. Then if you want to talk some more…'

'Gosh, Grace, are you that worried about me?'

'I'm a bit worried. You look like you're not sleeping, and not quite well. You look…pooky.'

'Pooky?'

'It's a technical term.'

Christina laughed. 'It'd be nice if you stayed over. Just so the house doesn't feel so empty. But you can have Joe's—' She stopped. Corrected herself. 'The spare room. No need for the couch. The bed's all made up in there.'

She'd washed the sheets yesterday, had left the bed unmade during the day then prepared the room ready for Megan in the evening, even though Megan wouldn't be moving in for another few days. Nice little strategy of pretending to herself that she was moving forward.

'And would there be an offer of hot Milo and a biscuit as well, by any chance?'

'In case I need another cry on Auntie Grace's shoulder while we're drinking it?'

'Thanks to the nightly Milo and biscuit, it's a pretty well-padded shoulder. You have to admit it's well suited for the purpose.'

Having Grace there overnight meant that she was still there in the morning, and in the morning Christina got out of bed feeling fine, but felt nauseous by the time she reached the bathroom and was retching into the basin by the time she'd got the lid off the toothpaste for a freshening of her mouth. She hadn't even shut the bathroom door.

Little weatherboard Queenslander cottages didn't have

very good soundproofing. Christina had rinsed her mouth out with plain water, since the toothpaste smelled way too strong and didn't seem like a very good idea. She was wiping her face with a towel, wondering why she still felt so funny in the stomach, why she'd been feeling this way for days, if she thought about it, when Grace appeared.

'What was that? Are you OK?'

'Not sure.' Although she'd begun to have an idea.

'Did you have very much to drink last night?'

'Half a glass of wine with Brian. Lemon squash at the party.'

Grace asked a couple more questions.

Christina answered them.

'I'm a midwife and you're a doctor,' Grace said. 'What do you think?'

They looked at each other.

Christina said, 'No.'

'No?'

Grace asked another set of questions.

Christina said, 'No,' again, but more desperately this time.

'We're going to do a test,' Grace decreed. 'I am zipping to the pharmacy this second, and we are doing a test.' She looked at her watch. 'They'll be open.' Being the only one in Crocodile Creek, the pharmacy had extended hours. 'It's after seven. What time do you have to get to the airport?'

'Not until eight. We have a scheduled patient transport this morning, and another one this...aagh... this afternoon.'

'Uh-oh, are you leaning over that basin again?'

'Yup.'

'I'll get you some dry biscuits. Or fruit?'

'Biscuits,' Christina gasped. 'And water.'

Grace brought the biscuits and a filled glass, then left

the house, which felt very silent and still after she'd gone. The biscuits and water helped. Christina felt better. She managed a shower, towelled her body dry, ate another biscuit and looked at herself naked in the mirror.

She looked the same.

She didn't look pregnant.

But she probably was.

The dates added up. There had been that stomach upset a month ago which she'd told herself hadn't lasted long enough to compromise the effectiveness of her contraception, but... How much wishful thinking had lain behind that conclusion?

Did she *want* to be pregnant, then?

Oh, lord, what had she been thinking a month ago? That she could force a commitment from Joe if something like this happened?

No, that implied some serious thinking about pregnancy over the past few weeks, which didn't fit where her thoughts had focused at all. Biological clock, yes, actual state of pregnancy, no. So much had changed since then.

She was shaking, nauseous again.

And still naked.

She touched her breasts, remembering Joe's hands on them last night. Did they feel fuller? Maybe a little. Something went thud in her stomach. Grace would be back with that test any moment now, and pregnancy tests now only took a few minutes to yield a very reliable result. She got dressed quickly, while her mind flooded with questions.

What do I want? A false alarm? A way to pressure Joe? No.

Not that.

Two could play the solitary heroism game.

She'd have to tell him, of course, but she would make

it clear to him from the very beginning that his involvement was not required.

A VW Beetle engine died noisily in her driveway and the front door opened thirty seconds later, while Christina was still in her bedroom. 'Here,' Grace said, handing over a paper bag from the pharmacy. 'I'm going to make you some breakfast. Toast and tea. Just show up for it when you're ready.'

'That'll be Christmas.'

Grace counted off the months on her fingers. 'Well, I guess by then I won't need to ask you the result of the test.'

Even without waiting until Christmas, she didn't need to ask Christina about the result of the test when Christina returned from the bathroom. Her whole face must have said positive.

'Oh, gosh! Oh, wow!' Grace breathed. 'Oh, I'm going to hug you!' She did. 'Oh, that's…momentous!'

'Yes,' Christina agreed shakily.

Understatement of the year. She still had no idea what this would mean, how it would change her attitudes or her plans. She couldn't focus at all. It didn't seem real, and yet at another level it felt *right*. She'd always known she wanted to be a mother, even if she'd never imagined it starting like this…

'Christina?'

'Hmm?' She blinked at her friend. She'd been miles away.

'When are you going to tell Joe?' Grace asked her gently.

CHAPTER NINE

Do we turn the flight around?

Christina looked at Jill and saw the same unspoken question reflected in the older nurse's face. This should have been a routine afternoon patient transport from the hospital back to this boy's isolated home on a cattle station in the Gulf country.

Ben was nine, in plaster from hip to toes after fracturing his femur falling from a horse, and he'd greeted them with a grin wider than his face, just after lunch, because he'd been so happy to be out of his hospital bed and going home with Mum to his dad and his sister. His mum had looked pretty happy about the whole thing, too, hugging him and getting dithery about packing up the get-well gifts he'd received.

'So much chocolate! The balloons are beautiful, but...'

'We don't let them on the plane,' Christina had had to tell her.

Forty minutes into the flight, Ben Cartwell wasn't grinning any more and Judy Cartwell wasn't thinking about balloons.

'I don't understand why this is happening, 'she said in a strained voice. She squeezed her son's hand. 'Just try and get your breath, Ben, try to relax. It's OK.'

The asthma attack had taken everyone by surprise. 'Mild asthma,' Mrs Cartwell had reported after the leg break, when staff had taken a patient history. But this attack wasn't mild. It had begun with an audible wheeze and moderate respiratory distress, and they'd quickly put up a nebuliser mask and given a dose of Ventolin, but if these were helping, they weren't helping enough.

'I've never seen him like this before,' Mrs Cartwell said. 'Ben, you don't have to be scared. Just relax.'

Turbulence rocked the aircraft once again, making equipment lockers rattle and stomachs swoop up and down. Christina didn't like the unpredictable motion any more than Ben did, and was beginning to wish she had a supply of those nice dry biscuits with her that Grace had found in the pantry this morning.

Speaking of which, Joe knew nothing about the pregnancy yet. She didn't know when she'd get the right opportunity to tell him, and she hated having to wait like this. It gave her too much time to plan out conversations that wouldn't work in real life the way they did in her head, because important conversations never did.

And was talking enough, anyhow? She craved action, but didn't know what she could do.

'This was what started it,' Jill murmured. 'It's very rough. He got scared, and that can be a strong trigger.'

'Glenn?' Christina said into her headset. 'What's the story? Do we know what weather we're coming into? More rough stuff?'

'Good chance,' Glenn answered. 'I could try flying higher.'

Jill and Christina looked at each other again. Fly higher, yes, but away from hospital care?

'What's happening?' Ben's mother wanted to know.

'What are we doing?' She sounded panicky herself, even though it was obvious she was trying not to. Ben could see the panic and it didn't help.

'How are you feeling, Ben?' Jill asked. Her voice was always much softer when she talked to a paediatric patient. 'Breathing better?'

As a highly experienced theatre nurse as well as the hospital's director of nursing, she didn't come on flight duty very often, but she liked to do it from time to time 'to keep my hand in', she said.

Grace was off today, so Jill had rostered herself for the two patient transport assignments, instead of sending another more junior nurse. That morning's trip had been quite uneventful, but Christina was grateful for Jill's level of experience right now.

You didn't want to turn a flight around for nothing. Like any medical service, this one operated on a budget that was always too tight, and flying cost money.

On the other hand...

Ben was shaking his head in answer to Jill. He tried to speak, but he couldn't. With his best, most desperate effort, nothing would come. Mrs Cartwell moaned in a shaky voice, 'Oh, Ben!'

Christina whipped her stethoscope back into her ears and practically glued the other end of it to Ben's chest, listening in several different places.

Silence. A layperson might have thought that the wheezing had stopped and that Ben's condition was improving. Christina knew better.

'Glenn, we're going to head back,' she yelled. 'Now, please. Ben, love, we'd better not take you home today after all. That's a disappointment, I know.'

But at the moment he was too distressed and frightened

to care. The aircraft lurched again as the boy kept up his panicky, desperate and futile efforts to breathe, half his face hidden by the misted mask of the nebuliser. His condition was worsening rapidly, his lungs almost completely closed. Fighting her queasy stomach, Christina found a pulse of almost 140, and a respiratory rate of forty-five. His trachea tugged inwards as he tried to breathe, using muscles that shouldn't need to be involved.

Jill had already begun to draw up the life-saving adrenaline he needed. 'Country nice and flat out here, Glenn?' she asked in a casual tone, and they all knew what she meant.

If Ben's condition didn't improve with this latest bar-rage of treatment and he arrested, they'd need to intubate him to maintain airway control, and that could only be done safely on the ground.

No, Christina resolved. By hook or by crook, she was going to bring this patient back from the brink before he got to that point.

'Flat? Yeah, mostly,' Glenn answered Jill, serious as ever. 'That's my problem, not yours.'

'Are we landing?' Mrs Cartwell said. 'Please, tell me what you're going to do for Ben.'

'We're heading back,' Jill said. 'Just for safety's sake.'

And, please, Christina added inwardly, let us not have to land in the middle of nowhere, on the way, so we can save this kid's life…

She had been hoping so strongly for a routine day. She would have been able to sign off at the end of it, drive across to the hospital from the flight base, find Joe, work out a time when they could talk. Nothing would make their conversation easy, but at least she'd have had some lead up, some preparation, a chance to stay calm. Now, even with the best-case scenario for Ben, she'd be jittery, awash with ebbing adrenaline, more tired than ever.

She felt the slow bank and lift of the aircraft as they turned back towards Crocodile Creek and gained some height. Jill gave the adrenaline. Christina listened to Ben's chest again, tried another dose of Ventolin. The turbulence eased.

And so, fractionally, did Ben's breathing, but he still looked desperately scared and struggling. It was so hard watching a child unable to breathe, and the time remaining until they would be back on the ground stretched ahead too far.

'Pulse rate has dropped a bit,' Jill reported. 'One-thirty. Respiratory rate at thirty-five now.' She raised her voice. 'Ben, love, you're doing a lot better. It might not feel that way yet, but you're getting better. Your chest is opening up again. Good lad!'

'We're doing the right thing, heading in this direction,' Christina said.

'Oh, absolutely!'

Their descent began at last, bumpy for most of the way. Even in the midst of his distress, Ben flinched every time, and Christina realised he was frightened about his leg.

'Your cast's protecting the break,' she told him. 'It's not going to go crooked, and it's not going to hurt.'

She wasn't sure that he believed her. His knuckles were white as he gripped his mother's hand, and she looked ill with fear.

On the ground, they made the transfer between aircraft and ambulance, and from the ambulance to the ED, with the boy's condition still touch and go.

Joe was working today, and things were busy. He always looked so energised and focused under these conditions, his big body moving efficiently, no hint of clumsiness or unnecessary noise. He turned away from an elderly woman who'd apparently taken a fall, saw the new stretcher being wheeled in, and saw Christina, too.

Be right with you, he gestured, but didn't spare the time for a smile.

My baby's going to look like him, Christina thought suddenly.

'This is a bounce,' she told him, as soon as Ben had been set up in an emergency cubicle. She meant that this patient had been discharged and had needed to come back. Joe understood the medical slang at once, and made a characteristic face. Bounce, hey? It never looked good for a hospital to have too many of those!

'Unrelated problem, though,' he said. 'Bad luck for the kid.'

'Mum's upset, too.'

'She would be!'

Joe checked Ben's vital signs. His oxygen saturation had climbed to ninety-four per cent now. There was no sign of cyanosis, no use of accessory muscles to breathe, and Ben could speak a full sentence. He'd need an oral steroid drug and monitoring for at least twenty-four hours.

'You're off the hook now,' Joe said to Christina.

'I know...' She was aware that she'd been hanging back, fiddling with Ben's notes, not really required now that the hospital staff had taken over. But she had to tell Joe that she wanted to see him. She saw Hamish coming towards them and grabbed her last chance. 'We need to talk, Joe.'

He looked at her, gave a half a smile at last. 'This talking stuff is getting to be a very bad habit between us, Tink,' he muttered.

'I know, but something's come up.' My stomach this morning, and a distinctive colour in a test window.

'I'm working a long shift today. Midnight.' And he'd be working again all day tomorrow, and flying back to Auckland early on Sunday morning. Christina was on call all weekend for emergency flights in the helicopter. How did you schedule a pregnancy conversation into a timetable like that?

And how did you follow through? She wouldn't see him for three weeks after this. From experience, she knew he was unlikely to phone. Three weeks was a long time when you'd just found out you were pregnant and didn't know what the baby's father would want.

I have to take action on this, she thought again.

'Hello, Ben,' Hamish said behind them. 'And this is Mum? Of course it is! I'm Dr McGregor.'

'Could you phone me at home, Joe?' Christina said. 'Let me know when you're about to take a dinner-break. I'll meet you somewhere.'

'I'll phone from the house and you can meet me there.'

'Let me have a wee chat to Dr Barrett,' they both heard from Hamish.

He was already coming their way. Joe's suggestion would have to do, because Christina couldn't come up with a better alternative in the middle of the ED.

She spent several agonising hours waiting at home, before reaching the earliest time at which she could expect Joe to call, and then she had to wait two hours more before he actually did, at nine o'clock. She knew it wasn't his fault, but it didn't improve her state of mind.

'I'm at the house.' Background sound half drowned his words. 'It's noisy, unfortunately.'

'I'll be right there.'

'Come along the veranda. Because if you go in through the kitchen…' Most people did, but you could get waylaid there with offers of tea or beer and never escape.

He sounded tense—irritated, probably—and she wondered what he'd picked up from her. That she was the kind of ex-lover destined to remain a nuisance?

Yes! With bells on!

'Want something to drink?' he offered when she got there.

'No, thanks.'

'I've got my dinner heating up in the microwave. I can't hang around here too long, Tink.' He said it gently, but he meant it. She felt like a nuisance again, even when he reached out and touched her shoulder, as if in apology. 'Half an hour at the most, and I have to get back.'

'That's OK,' she said. 'Get your dinner.'

He nodded and left. Christina heard voices in various parts of the house and hoped that no one knew she was there.

Joe's room felt too small with both doors shut and Christina already very on edge. She saw the flowers she'd picked for him on Sunday. They'd wilted by this time, and though the clear glass vase she could see their water had turned to a revolting cloudy beige. Her stomach had something to say about the sight.

Turning away from it, she looked at the bed, too hastily made. She could imagine his big body there, rumpled from sleep, warm, smelling just the way it should.

Joe came back with his dinner. 'This is horrible,' he announced.

'The meal?' It was one of those frozen things. He put it down on the desk next to the wilted flowers and didn't make any attempt to eat it.

'No, eating in front of you, rushing this.' He paused. 'Whatever it is.'

'It's…' As on Sunday night, she just had to say it. Creeping up on the subject—*Hey, guess what, I'm going to be shopping for a whole new wardrobe in about three months, Joe*—would be ridiculous. 'It's…'

Simple.

Only it wasn't.

'I'm pregnant, Joe.'

'Say that again?'

But she didn't. She knew he'd heard. He let out a low, rough sound, then made a jerky grab for the desk without looking at it. He hit the plate and it tipped over the desk edge and his dinner splattered onto the polished wooden floor. The plate bounced but didn't break, and landed on top of the food. They both looked at the mess helplessly in silence, then Joe gulped back a tortured laugh. 'Looked pretty inedible even before.'

'I'm sorry.'

She couldn't take this. Not the dinner. Not the vase water. Not Joe's reaction. She fled to the veranda and then on to the lush garden endowed by one of Charles Wetherby's forebears. She knew Joe would follow her, and it was a place that offered some potential privacy, if only behind screens of leaves.

He did follow, and she felt him behind her, watching and waiting until several deep, careful breaths had brought her nausea back under control. Was she going to feel this way for the next two months, or was it stress and fatigue as much as pregnancy?

'OK now?' he asked.

'Think so.'

She heard him sigh heavily between his teeth and turned to face him. She wanted to see what was written there, not imagine the worst. A cluster of frangipani leaves brushed his shoulder unnoticed, and he looked blank, struggling for steady ground, naked in his shock.

Which was probably better than pretending he was instantly happy.

Maybe it was better.

'Say something,' she prompted.

'I'm a bit stunned.'

'Yeah. And?' It sounded too hostile, too aggressive. Without waiting for an answer, she gabbled on, 'I was stunned, too. I'm not saying that it's an unacceptable response, first up.'

'If you were stunned, then you obviously didn't...' He stopped.

She knew what he'd been about to say. 'I didn't let it happen it on purpose?'

'I'm not suggesting it, Christina.'

Her body burned, and she felt compelled towards total honesty. 'You probably have a right to suggest it,' she told him in a low voice. She saw his eyes narrow, and went on quickly, 'Remember that stomach upset? Not to get too technical on the timing, but if I'd been really on the ball I would have taken a morning-after pill the day you flew out.'

'Did you think about it?'

She nodded. 'Coming home from the airport. But I thought the risk was very low.' She took a breath. 'And then I thought that even if it happened, would it be so terrible?'

Is it so terrible, Joe?

'So did you know about it on Sunday when you picked me up?' He reached up and began to shred the leaves with mechanical precision.

'No, of course not. You mean when I told you I'd arranged the room for you at the house? Of course not! Why?'

'I thought you might have been saving it up.'

'Saving it up?' she echoed blankly, before she understood what he meant. 'Oh, for heaven's sake! You mean like ammunition? A last-ditch stand?'

He whooshed out another sigh. 'That sounded bad, didn't it?'

'Yes. Very. If you really think I'm that—'

'Manipulative,' he cut in. 'I don't. I *don't.*'

'Then why say it?'

'Because I'm taking this as it comes, Tink. I didn't think you'd want pretence.' Well, he'd got that right, at least. 'Tell me…tell me what you're thinking and feeling. What you expect.' He added the last three words as if they cut his mouth.

'I don't expect anything. From you, you mean? Nothing! Only what you want. Support for my decision to keep the baby, that's all. Which was pretty instant, I should tell you.'

'Because I can't—I'm fighting to keep my head above water as it is.'

'I know that. You're hating this. It's got you terrified. This is worse than I expected, Joe.'

He threw the shredded leaves away and began to prowl back and forth. She went up to him and pinned him in place with her touch, and they managed to sit down next to each other on the ornamental garden seat. He leaned forward, resting his elbows on his knees, picking the green leaf matter from under his fingernails. He didn't say anything at first, and something told her she should simply wait.

'I was sixteen when Amber was born,' he said finally after several restless shifts of his shoulders and his legs. 'Old enough to realise straight away, and to get told, that something wasn't right. She was little and frail with such a strange, funny little face. She already had the trach in, of course, and an NG tube, and she was like…'

He stopped and shook his head, while Christina waited.

'When I was much younger, seven or eight,' he tried again, 'I rescued some baby birds from a nest that a cat had got to. They were still pink and featherless, just a day or two old, and of course they died. I couldn't manage to keep them warm or fed. And I just wasn't going to let the same thing happen to Amber. I just wasn't.'

'No…'

'Her face reminded me of those birds. Not the right shape. So naked and small. I felt so protective towards her. One of my best friends said something about her being a retard and I punched him in the stomach. Four times. This probably isn't explaining why I'm reacting this way now.'

He twisted towards her and their shoulders touched.

'I don't know if it is,' Christina said, close to tears. 'All I know is that you've had two years to tell me these stories. Now you expect me to catch up in a couple of days, understand everything about who you are, because of your life and your past, in a few days. When I've never seen where you live, met your family, heard any of this before. You're asking too much of me, Joe!'

'Yeah, that's ironic, isn't it? That's half of what I was trying to avoid. Asking too much of you.'

'And what's the other half?'

'Of what I'm trying to avoid? A horrible marriage like my mother and Geoff have. And the agony of being ready and waiting to cut off your own arm for the sake of someone you love. We were confronted with that so often in Amber's first few years of life. Time and time again I used to think, Today? Is today the day I should cut off the arm? I'm ready. Give me the signal. I mean, the thinking wasn't as concrete as that, but the feeling was there.'

'You think you're going to have to cut off your arm for me? For the baby?'

He didn't answer for a long time. 'I think I'm just tired,' he finally said.

And he needed to get back to the hospital, which meant a peanut-butter sandwich eaten standing up in the kitchen first, because his hot dinner was still splattered on the floor. 'So you should go,' she told him. 'I'll clean up.'

'Don't. I mean it, Christina. I'll be really angry if you do.'

She left it where it was.

The congealed microwave meal was still on the floor when Joe got back to his room just after midnight. He looked at it, glad that Christina had taken him seriously and hadn't cleaned it up. He unglued the plate from on top of it, tried to remember what the packet had claimed the meal to be, but couldn't. With a handful of paper towel, he scooped most of it up and chucked it in the bin. Several passes with a cleaning sponge took care of the rest.

The ED had been busy again that night, with a procession of routine cases, including a couple of difficult types—a bad-tempered drunk who'd aspirated some of his own stomach contents, a heroin overdose whose family situation would need looking into. Christina's asthma patient Ben had gone up to the paediatric ward, his chest in pretty good shape considering how bad he'd been earlier, but a question mark still hanging over the issue of his discharge after the period of observation. He seemed very nervous about another flight. Sedation was probably the best option.

Joe had looked in on Jim Cooper, too, even though he was listed as Gina's patient now. He'd brewed up a mild infection which had slowed his recovery over the past couple of days. Honey split her time between her husband and her daughter, while remaining fiercely protective of Jim's ignorance about the baby.

'Not until he's ready!'

Meanwhile, Honey fretted about whether the dogs and the other animals were really being taken care of properly by whatever help Charles had organised out there.

Hungry after such a long day but definitely not wanting another microwave meal, Joe prowled into the kitchen. No one was there. The house was very quiet. He peered into the fridge and found some Cheddar cheese on one of the crowded shelves. There was even some bread left. Cheese on toast. That would do.

Communal living wasn't his favourite thing, even though everyone in this place was pretty good. Moodiness was kept private, boundaries were respected. Food kitty money was usually paid, shopping and cleaning rosters were adhered to, and quite often someone cooked a big meal.

But he had a need for privacy and solitude that couldn't be fully met here. He also had a need to know that if he left three slices of cold pizza in the fridge overnight, they'd still be there the next day to heat up when he came in from a long stint at the hospital and wanted some supper. His life wasn't simple, so he seized on simplicity wherever he could find it, even in the little things—like where his next meal was coming from.

He'd been pushing himself too hard for such a long time. He'd worked long part-time hours while he'd studied medicine. He had a full patient load in his practice, squeezed into three weeks out of four. He worked as many hours as Charles Wetherby would let him when he was here, bracketed on either side by flights of several hours across the Tasman Sea and boring waits at airports in Brisbane or Cairns.

He'd pretended to Christina through their whole relationship. Pretended that he was this laid-back, carefree, relaxed kind of guy. Hell, it had been so good! But it had been
a pretence. In his real life, there was no room for carefree
or relaxed. He wished there was. He wished he could open
up that part of him and let it fly, the way he'd been able to
do here, with Christina…the way she'd told him wasn't
enough for her any more.

'What do I smell?' said Mike Poulos, behind him.

'I can make some more,' Joe offered at once, hiding the
fact that he'd rather eat alone.

'It's fine. I just wanted some water.' Mike found a
chilled jug of it in the drinks fridge, and soon disappeared
again. He should have been Christina—because she was
the only person in Crocodile Creek Joe wanted to share a
fridge with—but he wasn't.

Joe would be on a plane to Auckland in thirty hours. His
flight would get in late in the afternoon, and he had patients
to see in his group general practice on Monday morning,
starting at nine and going through until seven. Later in the
week, Amber had a medical appointment to talk about the
jaw surgery that her doctors wanted to perform soon.

He and Mum and Geoff would all be present at the appointment as well. There was still some uncertainty about
whether they'd be able to remove Amber's tracheostomy
at this point, and Geoff would no doubt get belligerent
about it. How come these supposed experts didn't have definitive answers? How come it would still take so many
more procedures to get Amber looking 'right'?

'Joe, tell these idiots!' Geoff would no doubt say.
'You're a doctor! They won't talk down to you like they
talk down to me!'

And back here in Crocodile Creek, Joe's own child

would be quietly growing in Christina's womb. Healthy? You had to believe so. You couldn't spend seven months or more being scared. But even the smoothest pregnancy in the world was tough to go through alone.

He felt as if someone was tearing him in two, and hated Fate for the trick it had played. He'd got himself into this situation because he'd so badly wanted time out and fun, something that was just simple and good, and now he'd ended up with more responsibility than ever.

Even if he stopped coming to Crocodile Creek out of sheer self-protection, if he never saw Christina again and never met their child, he would always know, always wonder. Boy or girl? Bright? Athletic? Artist, scientist, dreamer? Like me, or like her? He'd always know that someday Christina or the child might need or want to make contact.

At which point, he would be confronted with everything he'd put Christina through, and everything he'd missed out on.

He didn't know what to do.

Christina couldn't get to sleep, even though she was once again exhausted to the point of nausea. She found a packet of sea-salted chips in the pantry and the salt settled her stomach but not her stress levels.

She had meant what she'd said to Joe earlier. It hadn't helped their situation at this point that he'd held so much back over the past two years. That story about Amber and the baby birds… You couldn't doubt his intensity, his sincerity, but a summary of his life at home and a couple of anecdotes weren't enough.

She gave up even trying to get to sleep, went on the internet and did another search on Treacher Collins syndrome. The first time, she'd done a search of the whole Web, but this time she clicked the 'pages from Australia' button.

And suddenly, after scrolling through several screens and clinking on various links, she saw Joe himself smiling out at her in close-up, his mouth wide, his teeth very white in his bronzed face, his strong arms wrapping from behind around the shoulders of a girl who looked about twelve or thirteen.

Amber.

She was smiling, too, her trach kept in place at her throat by a plastic strap that looked like a white necklace.

Christina couldn't believe it at first. It didn't seem real, to discover Joe and his sister this way, to think that if she'd had any reason to explore TCS on the internet over the past couple of years she might have stumbled on them like this before she'd ever heard about Amber from Joe.

Why hadn't he mentioned this site to her?

Why hadn't he mentioned the poem that Amber had written?

'"I am not quite like you",' she had called it, and then the lines had gone on to describe feelings and tastes and day-to-day routines that were exactly like those of thousands of other young girls, interspersed with stark descriptions of things that were very different.

'When I wake in the night, haunted by a scary dream, I scream.
But it is silent. I have my trach. My breathing does not touch my voice.'

Christina read the poem and looked at Joe and Amber until the computer screen switched to sleep mode and went dark. She didn't know how long she might have gone on sitting there if it had stayed bright.

All night?

She knew what she wanted to do now. She just didn't know how far Charles Wetherby would be willing to go to make it possible. She'd have to see him in the morning, as early as she could.

CHAPTER TEN

THE morning felt a lot fresher than Joe himself did as he walked across to the hospital just seven hours after he'd left it.

He had a mug of coffee in one hand and a piece of stale Danish pastry in the other, because there were too many people already in the kitchen at the doctors' house, making breakfast, and he'd had to escape some well-meaning questions from people that he just didn't have it in him to fob off today.

In the quiet of a Saturday morning he could hear the waves lapping gently in the cove and some parrots squabbling in the trees. There was another sound, too, that took a few seconds to penetrate his consciousness and announce its identity. It was a low throb, getting louder.

It was the rescue chopper.

He saw it rise over the top of the hospital, coming from the helipad, which wasn't visible from where he stood. It swung out towards the dark turquoise carpet of ocean, hanging at an angle in the sky in a fashion which reminded him of how glad he was that he only ever had to go out in it on the rarest occasions—just twice, during the two years he'd been coming here.

Christina flew in it almost every week.

She was probably flying in it now.

The issue wasn't courage, it was trust. She had more trust than he did—trust in other people's competence, their good intentions, their strength. Trust in *him,* for that matter, more than he had in himself. Would he really get it remotely right with his response to this baby, who didn't yet seem real? Yes, she had too much trust, he sometimes thought... And he felt much happier when the whirly-bird rotor-blades had levelled off parallel with the horizon and the thing was at least flying straight.

It rose higher, travelling over the water, and headed directly out to sea. The Great Barrier Reef lay in that direction, roughly thirty kilometres offshore. Less than a third of that distance away floated Wallaby Island, home to one of the Reef's most extensive tourist resorts. This was its peak season, with holidaymakers going there for a break from the much harsher winter down south. The rescue chopper could easily be headed there, or to one of the other tourist islands further to the north or south. It had almost disappeared by the time Joe entered the main hospital building.

He started straight in on a morning round, wanting to fit it in before the inevitable call to the ED, where he would be mainly working again that day. In the paediatric ward, he found Cal Jamieson checking on Shane's appendicectomy incision, his pain levels and his notes.

'We'll get him off the morphine,' Cal told a nurse. 'He's looking good.'

Ben was in the next bed, his breathing further improved and his observations also better than they had been yesterday afternoon. Joe talked to his mother about giving a sedative tomorrow before they even mentioned that he'd be taking a flight home, and she nodded. 'I think that would help. Nothing too strong, though.'

'You don't have to worry, Mrs Cartwell.'

He saw a couple of other people then headed in the direction of the ED. Georgie Turner collared him on the way, striding up behind him and calling his name. Her short black hair looked sleek and shiny and she had way too much energy for a single parent who regularly got called out at odd hours to bring other people's babies into the world.

Christina's baby, in about seven and a half months?

Would he be there? Did he want to be? Would she accept him at that point?

'Listen, Joe, Christina was going to show Megan and her mother the room at her place this morning,' Georgie said, 'but she's been called out on an emergency flight to one of the islands.'

'Not Wallaby?'

'No, further than that. There was a question about needing to refuel, I think, and we don't know how long they'll be.'

'I saw the chopper going out,' Joe confirmed. 'Not that long ago.'

'She called in a message for you, in mid-air. Apparently you know where she keeps her spare key?'

'Yep,' he answered stoically, while his gut turned sour.

'Can you grab a break at some point and take Megan and her mother over there? Charles has OK'd a hospital car. He'll give you the keys for it. There are a couple of boxes of donated gear for them to take as well. It should only take half an hour or so. They just want to look around and see if the place'll work. But you know the house.'

He nodded, and Georgie made an apologetic face.

'It's gorgeous,' she continued. 'So I'm sure Megan will love it.'

'Shouldn't be a problem. Shall I phone the unit when I'm ready?'

'Sounds good. Thanks, Joe.' She walked briskly back the way she'd come.

In the ED he saw a couple of patients, ordered an X-ray on one and an ultrasound on the other. Emily was floating around as well. She glanced into the almost empty waiting room when he mentioned Megan and her mother, and suggested, 'Tell them you'll go now. We have no one coming in, other than our chopper case, and they won't get here for at least another few hours.'

'So you know where they were going, do you?'

'York Island. Fair distance.'

'Know why?'

'Didn't hear so, yes, they might be ages, depending on how much they need to stabilise the patient on the ground.'

Christina could be gone for most of the day. They'd probably see each other when she got back. She would be bringing a patient in. Shark attack, near drowning, heart problem, fishing accident, it could be anything. He might not hear any detail for a while. When she got here, they'd be snapping information and questions and instructions back and forth to each other, a glance and a word or two the only personal interaction.

He'd have to watch her holding everything together when she was tired and tense. They might get separated altogether by the demands of the day. She could get called out again tonight, or he might have to assist in surgery. His flight left next morning at six, which meant getting up in the dark, tiptoeing around the doctors' house, getting his last-minute gear together…

Hell, they might not see each other at all.

But we can't leave it like this, he thought. I have to tell her...

What? That she wasn't on her own? When he still didn't know how much he could honestly promise? He still felt weighed down. And he didn't want to lie to her.

He felt Emily's concerned eyes fixed on him. 'Everything OK, Joe?'

'Yep. Fine. You're right. Let me deal with Megan and her mother now, in case there isn't a better chance later.'

'Yes, because Christina is apparently keen to get it settled today. I'll phone the unit and make sure they're ready.'

He was told that they were, but when he got there he found that this had been an optimistic assessment. Honey was still going through the boxes of donated gear, which had been brought from Jill's office. 'You won't need this for him here,' she told her daughter.

'I might,' Megan said. 'For a coming-home outfit.'

She held up the ridiculously tiny garment and smiled at it. Both mother and daughter looked a lot happier and more relaxed than they had a few days ago.

Jackson lay sleeping nearby in his premmie cot, with its transparent sides. Megan looked at him, frowning. 'What if he wakes up for a feed?'

'He had a good one an hour ago.'

'But he sometimes doesn't go much longer than that, Mum.' Like all new mothers, she was already the person who knew more about her baby than anyone else.

'You have some expressed milk in the fridge,' a nurse reassured her. 'We can give him that.'

'Ready?' Joe suggested.

But Honey was still going through the last box. 'Five minutes?'

He knew he'd better call the ED, check that this outing

was still OK. He could envisage it getting extended at the other end, too. Waiting for Emily to come to the phone, he saw a slow, careful figure enter the doorway. Gown-clad, wheeling a drip stand, rather frail despite his wiry build…

Crikey, it was Jim Cooper.

No one else in the room had seen him yet.

The phone rattled in Joe's ear and he heard Emily's voice. 'Problem?'

'Just that we haven't gone yet.'

'That's OK. It's still quiet down here,' Emily said.

'Good. Great. Bye.'

'Joe—?'

But he put down the phone, cutting her off, wondering if he could or should try and head off the imminent confrontation. Jim had seen his daughter. He was smiling, because he could see how good she looked. She'd been to his room to see him a couple of days ago, Joe knew, but apparently she'd acted cagey and distant, hiding behind the fact that Jim had still been pretty weak and ill at that stage. Honey had supported her daughter's secrecy.

'She'll come again when you're better,' she'd told her husband.

'And you're not to try and come to see me,' Megan had told him, but two days later he felt strong enough, and it was clearly a very innocent defiance of his wife and daughter's prohibition.

Jim found Honey, still hovering over that wretched box of donations, and called out, 'Love? Couldn't think where you'd got to. Decided it was time I came to see my girl, under my own—'

He stopped.

He'd seen the baby in the clear-sided little cot.

And hospitals didn't park a tiny newborn—one who

was still attached to various bits of tubing—that close to someone who wasn't the mother.

Five people froze.

Predictably, Honey was the first to react.

'Just don't upset yourself, Jim.' She hurried forward, wringing another tiny baby garment into sweaty pleats in her hands without even knowing it was there. 'She didn't want to tell you. Didn't tell me for days. She had him at the rodeo, and she thought he was stillborn. It's a miracle he's alive, and doing so well. He's got a blood disorder, but it's all right now that we know about it. The birth is why she was so ill. She's keeping him. We're grandparents. I know you're going to be thrilled. A boy, Jim!' Her tone begged him to see the baby's existence her way. 'There's a boy in the family! Just don't upset yourself!'

She put her arms around him tightly. As if she was afraid he would fall? Or afraid he'd lash out? Joe had heard he had a temper, but not that he might be violent.

He wasn't violent.

He didn't have the intent, or the strength.

'Get me a chair,' he told his wife hoarsely. 'How could she be pregnant?'

'She—'

'It was the boy. Was it?'

'Jack? The father? Of course he is!'

'I sent him away. And his uncle sacked him. Damn that man…damn that man.'

'Mr Cooper, let's try to stay quiet, OK?' Joe came in.

The man was shaking, and his breathing was shallow. He needed a bypass sooner rather than later, and he had just made his hand into a fist and pressed it against his heart— The gesture sent out warning bells.

'Jim, are you in pain?' Joe tried again.

'No. No. Just…can't get my breath. It's nothing.'

Joe didn't wait. There was oxygen equipment already in the room. 'Wheelchair,' he said to the nurse, while he found a mask and prepared the flow. 'We'll put him on the portable supply and get him back to his own room, where we can look after him properly.' A minute later, they had Jim in the chair and Joe stood behind him, ready to push the wheelchair himself.

'I'm coming, Jim,' Honey said. She lowered her voice. 'Megan, the house visit will have to wait.'

'I know that. It doesn't matter.'

'Dr Farrelly wanted to get it settled today.'

'Don't fret, Mum.'

'You're a fine one to talk!'

Jim breathed noisily through the mask.

'Does he realise?' Megan continued, her distressed whisper louder than she knew. 'Does he understand? Is that why he's—? Does he understand that I won't be coming home?'

'Didn't even get to see the little bloke properly,' Jim complained a few minutes later, back in his own hospital bed.

'Jim…' Honey said.

'I know. All right? I heard, back there with Megan, and I know this is the end. I know we can't manage, just the two of us, and I know she won't want to come back. Can't come back. Not until the little fella's stronger anyway, and by then it'll be too late.'

'She thinks she's broken your heart, love. She was so scared to tell you. She wouldn't let me talk about it, prepare you, say anything at all, and then when we saw you looking at him… She's called him Jackson… I think she really loves the Ransome boy, Jim.'

'Lot of good that's going to do her, since he hasn't shown his face in six months.'

Honey fell silent and her head drooped. 'Yes, that's a disappointment.'

'We'll put the place on the market as soon as we can. We won't get enough for it, not nearly enough, with the state it's in, but we can set ourselves up in town. I can get work. There'll be something. It's not the end of the world. Doesn't Megan know that?'

'Jim, she thinks she's broken your heart.'

'No, Honey, love,' Jim said, his voice creaking with bone-deep fatigue. 'That happened a long time ago.'

Joe was still finishing up an addition to Jim's notes when Charles Wetherby arrived to see his childhood friend.

'I heard you gave us another scare just now,' he said.

'Someone has to keep you on the ball, Charlie,' Jim answered.

'Trust me, there's plenty happens around here to do that!'

Jim managed a half-hearted grin at Charles, but then Joe saw the expression drain from his face as he looked at the doorway. 'You!'

Charles turned, but before he could speak, Philip Wetherby—because this had to be Philip Wetherby, even though Joe hadn't encountered Charles's brother before—told him, 'I've been trying to catch up to you the whole way along the corridor. You move way too fast in that thing, and I've been driving half the night from the property. I called out, but you didn't hear.'

'Did Lynley send you, Philip?'

'No. Hell, no! I thought we needed to talk about this face to face.'

'Right. In other words, not in front of your wife?'

'That's right,' he agreed with a hunted look.

'Do you want to see me in my office?'

The younger Wetherby hesitated, giving Charles the opportunity to pounce.

'On second thoughts, whatever you've got to say, say it here. It's appropriate, with the three of us.'

'I'll catch you later, Charles,' Joe said quickly, but Charles clamped a hand on his arm as he started past the wheelchair.

'Hang about, if you don't mind, Joe,' the medical administrator said mildly. 'Think it might be handy for us to have a witness to this.'

'Sure,' he agreed carefully.

'Thanks.' Charles looked up at his brother, in no way diminished by his lesser height in the chair. 'Speak, Philip.'

Philip tightened his already narrow lips. 'It's pretty simple. I'm here to tell you that you win, Charles.'

Charles merely raised his eyebrows.

'You know what I'm saying. There's no need to force the sale. I'll do what has to be done.'

'Are you listening to this, Jim?' Charles said.

'Yeah, but I want it spelled out, if it's what I think.'

'I'll grant the access to Gunya Creek. But I won't tell Lynley the truth. That Jim didn't pull the trigger. And no one else is to be told either. You and Jim have always agreed you were just as much to blame, horsing around, not paying any attention, calling me the gun-bearer and sticking me with the guns and all the work. I was thirteen! And I think you're wrong that it should have been dealt with after Dad died. By then it was water under the bridge.'

'Not for the Coopers.'

'Do we have to?'

Charles cut his brother off. 'You continued to exact a

punishment that our father put in place at a point where it made sense for Jim and me to protect you. And, yes, I'll admit we were protecting our own backsides, too, because we knew Dad's retaliation might have been even more extreme if he'd known how careless we all were. He was a violent man. But when Dad died, your "standing in the community" wasn't an excuse, Philip.'

'Do we need to cover this ground? I've said I'll do what you want, as long as my wife doesn't have to know.'

'Because of her "standing in the community"?'

'Pretty much.'

'The creek access isn't enough. It would have been ten years ago, but it's not any more. Wetherby Downs is going to give Jim and Honey everything they need to get back on their feet, little brother, or the sale goes ahead. Restocking, equipment, labour to ride their fences and deliver their feed, until they're back in profit.'

'I'll have to work out a budget.'

'The money's there.'

'It is,' Philip conceded.

'So the budget isn't necessary. And there's one more thing.'

Philip pressed his fingers over his eyes. 'How can there be more? Isn't this enough?'

'This one won't threaten your ego too much,' Charles promised in a mild tone. 'I'd just like you to find out where that nephew of ours has got to, if you have any information.'

'Our nephew? You mean Jack?'

'Your sister Celia's boy, Philip,' Jim said. 'Took weeks for Honey and me to find out his last name was Ransome.'

'Yes, born and raised in Sydney,' Philip answered, 'and then Celia tells me he wants to be a cattleman and can I please train him up.' He shook his head. 'You surely can't hold me responsible for what happened with your daughter, Cooper. They were both over eighteen.'

'Yeah, and now they're both parents,' Jim said softly. The new light of hope that had appeared in his eyes a few minutes ago was getting brighter. 'And call us naïve, Philip, but it might make a difference. We'd just like him to know.'

An hour out of Crocodile Creek, on the return flight, Mike Poulos radioed a report to Base about the patient they were bringing in. She was thirty-four, on a reef holiday with her husband, in early pregnancy and with a history of pelvic inflammatory disease. They received a confirmation that Dr Turner would be standing by for emergency surgery when they landed.

Because it had to be an ectopic pregnancy.

Knife-like abdominal pain on one side, bloating and spotting, signs of shock… Every symptom pointed to it, as well as the patient's history. Christina had broken the bad news and the woman and her husband were both upset, mourning the loss of a planned child and the risk to future fertility.

With her own pregnancy constantly in her mind, Christina ached for them but didn't let it get personal. It wouldn't help them to hear her own story, or to have her inwardly wondering how she'd feel in the same situation and whether there was any chance that Joe would be by her side—whether she'd want him if they had no future together.

During flight, the options for treatment were standard, straightforward and limited. They were treating the shock and buying time until the surgery, basically. Christina had given oxygen, IV fluids and pain medication, and elevated the patient's feet.

'Not long now,' she told the woman and her husband, seeing the shape of the coastline take on familiar lines.

'And did you catch that message for you from Charles?' Mike asked her. 'That he's got things sorted out for this week?'

'Yes, I got it, Mike,' she answered, not yet daring to think that this was good news.

On the ground, in the ED, Joe heard the sound of the chopper blades overhead, just as he had that morning on the Remote Rescue's outward flight.

'Do we know what this is yet?' he asked Emily.

He'd been all over the hospital that morning, both before and after that scene in Jim Cooper's room. He hadn't caught up on what kind of case was being brought in, whether they'd need him.

'The rescue chopper?' Emily was writing up some notes, and didn't look up from them. 'With Christina? She has an ectopic pregnancy. It's ruptured. Georgie's going to operate, with Jill assisting and I don't know who else. Apparently...'

The world faded. The sounds of the ward, the fluorescent light overhead.

All of it.

Just faded...

Joe blinked slowly. Emily had stopped speaking. He realised that suddenly she was looking at him, and although she'd been sitting half a second ago, she was now on her feet and standing close. 'Lord, Joe, what is it?'

'Nothing.' He whooshed out a breath, willing the room to stop spinning and those blotches in front of his eyes to disappear. 'Don't worry, it's nothing.'

Although Dr Morgan did have a certain way with words this week!

Resolving the ambiguity had only taken him a few seconds. It wasn't Christina's pregnancy that had lodged in a

Fallopian tube and ruptured the narrow passage. Good grief, of course it wasn't! She was bringing in a patient.

But in that brief time when he'd got it wrong…

'Are you sure, Joe?' Emily was still frowning at him. 'You look as if your whole life just passed before your eyes.'

'It did. But it's gone now. See? Whee!' He made his hands into butterfly wings. He did not want to talk about this!

What had talking really done for himself and Christina this week?

The ebb of the momentary burst of adrenaline left him way shakier and more distracted than he should have been. In the two seconds that had ticked by while he'd given Emily's words the wrong meaning, he'd mentally cancelled his flight home tomorrow, called the other doctors in his practice and arranged for them to cover his workload for the next week, even decided that Amber's appointment to talk about her surgery could be postponed, because helping Christina through the dangerous loss of her pregnancy was much more important. Anything that Christina wanted he would give her, because it was so important.

Important and a dragging weight of responsibility at the same time, but he couldn't let that stop him. Would she let him take it on, though, when he'd made it painfully clear to her this week how much of an added burden it would be? When he knew he wouldn't be able to hide the weight?

'I'm grabbing a two-minute coffee,' he told Emily.

'Are you really sure you're all right?'

'I'm fine.' He was going to be, as long as he could find some time with Christina today.

'Have you had lunch?'

'Not yet.'

'Take lunch, Joe.'

'It's OK.'

'Look, this new patient is going straight into surgery. Georgie's already here, waiting to scrub. If you want to talk to Christina, she'll be free in a few minutes.'

'What makes you think I want to talk to Christina?' Oh, lord, if this had become everyone else's business already, when he still didn't know what the outcome would be, he'd hate it.

'Because you said her name, Joe. Didn't you hear yourself?'

'No. Said her name?'

'Just now, when I told you about the incoming case. And you sounded as if it was part of your dying breath.'

His dying breath.

Joe lost count of how many of those he took over the next fifteen hours, but they all felt that way. It had to be some kind of cosmic punishment, he decided. He hadn't talked to Christina for two years, not about the things she'd wanted to hear. Now he was desperate to talk to her, but their paths just did not cross.

He was called to an emergency admission, and by the time he'd admitted and treated the burns case that had confronted him, Christina had gone out on another urgent flight. He should have been off in the evening, but Charles asked him if he could manage to stay late. 'We've got a staffing glitch suddenly for the coming week. I'm swapping a few people around. I…uh…shouldn't give you the details, I don't think.'

'No. Fine, Charles.' He blinked. Somebody else had had some confidential emergency. He should probably spare a bit of emotional energy, hoping everything was OK for them since the medical staff at Crocodile Creek had had their share of problems lately, but he couldn't. Spare emotional energy? There wasn't any. 'Yes, I can stay on as late as I'm needed,' he said.

When Christina returned with their latest patient—a truckie who'd overturned his vehicle and had a query head injury—Joe was busy, and when he thought about her in the quieter hours of the night, wondering if he could grab a break, phone her, go over for half an hour as long as he kept his pager clipped to his pocket, it just didn't seem to make sense.

One in the morning? She'd be fast asleep. You didn't waken a woman at that hour to promise you'd 'be there for her' when you knew you couldn't hide from her just how much the promise would cost.

Four-thirty in the morning... Honey was suddenly aware of someone in the room. She'd gone to sleep by Jim's side and now she woke up, her hand in his. But someone was there. She looked up and it was Megan.

'Just checking,' Megan said, and gave a half-smile that was tentative and fearful but still better than any smile Honey had seen for months. 'Dr Wetherby says Dad's going to be OK.'

'He is, love. And such good news. I can't believe we have access to the creek. The feud is over. We'll have money to restock. We can go home...'

'I don't know...'

'There'll be money for you to go to university now,' Honey told her, reaching out in the dim light to hold her daughter's hand. 'Maybe we have to wait until Jackson's a bit older but there are distance courses... You can study at home and do the access weekends... Somehow we'll work it out.'

'We surely will.' It was Jim, awake, his half-lidded eyes watching his wife and his daughter with a joy that shone through his drugged sleepiness.

'The first thing is your bypass, Dad,' Megan said.

'The first thing is your happiness,' Jim growled. 'Megan, girl, I'm so sorry... We asked too much from you. We'll make it up to you. You'll see.'

'I'll be fine, Dad,' she murmured. 'I'll be fine.'

Honey leaned forward and kissed her husband gently on the forehead. 'We'll all be fine now,' she murmured. 'We'll be a family.'

Would they? Megan gazed down at her parents and saw the love they felt for each other and felt her heart twist. It had been such a short time... Such a short time to know her heart...

Where was he?

He was out there, she thought. Somewhere, he was out there. Please.

There were footsteps in the corridor. She heard murmured talking and looked out to see Dr Farrelly and Dr Wetherby talking urgently in the corridor. Another drama?

But Charles was tugging Christina down to give her a swift hug, and Christina was carrying a holdall.

Megan closed her eyes. Christina was going to her love, she thought. That Kiwi doctor who'd been so nice this week. Her love... She knew it.

Someday I will, too, Jack, she promised. Someday I will, too.

It was still dark when Joe got up, after a bare three hours' sleep over at the house. He had his bag already packed, didn't feel like breakfast. His whole body creaked with stiffness and fatigue. He got to the airport at five-fifteen, every muscle in his body still moving with lead weights attached.

And there was Christina, when he thought he'd lost his

last chance to see her for three endless weeks. She'd come to see him off.

'Tink!'

With the airport lounge almost empty, he'd seen her straight away, standing near the check-in desk, waiting for him. She waved and smiled as he strode towards her, his heavy bag suddenly much lighter in his grip. His stiffness faded.

She stuck out a mile in his vision, the way she always had. She'd always seemed to him to have so much *more* than any other woman he'd ever met.

More heart.

More energy.

A more beautiful smile.

'Hi,' she said as he reached her, her voice husky.

'Tink,' he said again. He buried his face in her neck, inhaling the scent of her hair in open appreciation. 'Mmm, you smell so good!' And she was the only person who ever made him feel this way when he hugged her.

Tingling.

Exultant.

Where he belonged.

He couldn't help the relief and happiness he felt, even if it was an illusion, even if the weight came down hard on his shoulders again a minute from now. At least this way he'd get to tell her face to face that she wouldn't be going through pregnancy and parenthood alone.

'What are you doing here at this hour?' he asked her, trying to keep it light. 'Seeing me off?'

'Coming with you,' she said. Her mouth pressed hard against his hair, his cheekbone, the corner of his mouth. She held him tight. 'I'm flying to Auckland with you, Joe.'

'That's…not possible.'

'It is, thanks to Charles, who cleared my roster for the week, and to the airline, which fortunately had some spare seats.'

'Wh—?'

She was still smiling at him. No, she was grinning. Laughing into his face, stroking his jaw, looking happy and excited, like a tourist on her honeymoon.

Yes, and she had a packed bag at her feet.

His heart began to lift.

It shouldn't be doing that.

Why was it doing that?

It should be sinking like a stone, weighed down with his awareness of what she was prepared to give, with his re-sponsibility for her happiness if he let her give it. For hours he'd been expecting this sinking feeling, steeling himself against it, dreading it.

But now it wasn't happening. His heart wasn't sinking, it was lifting. Like a bird. Like a plane. Like…Superman? Except that he'd just begun to glimpse the possibility that he didn't have to be Superman any more.

'Because you said it yourself, Joe,' she said, speaking only for him. 'Sometimes talking isn't what counts. There has to be action.'

Her eyes were alight. Yes, she could see how he felt. See that weight lifting. See him about to float up in the air like an untethered balloon.

'So I stopped listening to what you said, and started thinking about everything you'd actually done over the past two years since we've been together. I know you love me,' she said, 'and I'm not letting this go. I'm not letting you shoulder everything on your own. You're not shoulder-ing anything on your own from now on, because you have me. I'm spending a week in New Zealand with you and your family while we make some plans for how we're going to handle our future *together*. I don't care about the details, if we live here or there, if we use my savings or keep them, but the *together* part is non-negotiable. I'm fighting for that. OK?'

Her eyes narrowed a little and she lifted her chin. He suddenly saw that she was a little less confident and bull-dozer-ish about this than she would have him believe, and that was unbearable. He couldn't let her suffer the doubt for another second.

'I love you,' he said, holding her tight. 'I love you and I want you, and you're right, I'm not letting you go. I'm fighting for it. You know what? I'm not reacting right.' He shook his light, giddy head, grinning. 'I never thought—Well, I never thought you'd do something like this. I thought we wouldn't see each other for three weeks and that when I came back it would go on being tough. But even if I'd expected you here this morning, saying what you've said, I would have thought it would make me feel…loaded down. Even more than before. And that I'd just drag you down, too.'

'That's why you wouldn't let me do it.' She understood.

'Yes. Only yesterday, something happened… it was stupid… When Emily said you were bringing in the ectopic pregnancy she worded it so that for a few seconds I thought the patient was you. And I knew in that instant that I'd drop everything to be with you, no matter what. And something clicked.'

'Yeah?' She pressed her nose against his.

'I was going to offer you everything, all my support. I was so glad to see you standing here, because it gave me the right chance to say it. But I thought it would feel as if I'd put the last nail in my own coffin. Only it's not making me feel that way. It's making me feel—Oh, lord, Tink, if you really want to do this…'

'Actions speak louder than words.' She waved her passport in his face. Through the terminal windows, the light of dawn had begun to seep higher and brighter in the eastern sky.

Joe laughed out loud. 'It feels good. It feels great. I'm…just happy. Christina Farrelly, I'm happy!'

'The way we've always felt when we're together, Joe,' she whispered. 'And it's not going to change.'

'You think?'

'I know! But I didn't know how to make you see it. Just telling you didn't help. I finally realised I had to show you. Take action. Prove it.'

'And let my reaction argue the case? It has, Tink. I'm—'

'Happy!' She grinned, then kissed him sweetly.

'Happy.'

'And about the baby?'

'So happy.'

She didn't seem to doubt him.

'I'm never going to let you go,' he whispered.

'We do have to check in.'

'Don't have to let you go to do that. I have skills. See?' He shouldered his bag and picked up her suitcase in the same hand, which left plenty of him still for her.

'Oh, Joe!' She laughed and grabbed his spare arm, and together, half an hour later, they took flight into the dawn, towards their shared future.

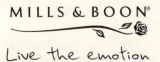

MILLS & BOON®

Live the emotion

MARCH 2006 HARDBACK TITLES

ROMANCE™

The Greek's Chosen Wife *Lynne Graham*	H6340	0 263 19134 6
Jack Riordan's Baby *Anne Mather*	H6341	0 263 19135 4
The Sheikh's Disobedient Bride *Jane Porter*		
	H6342	0 263 19136 2
Wife Against Her Will *Sara Craven*	H6343	0 263 19137 0
Bought for the Marriage Bed *Melanie Milburne*		
	H6344	0 263 19138 9
The Italian's Wedding Ultimatum *Kim Lawrence*		
	H6345	0 263 19139 7
The Innocent Virgin *Carole Mortimer*	H6346	0 263 19140 0
Ruthless Reunion *Elizabeth Power*	H6347	0 263 19141 9
The Cattle Baron's Bride *Margaret Way*	H6348	0 263 19142 7
The Cinderella Factor *Sophie Weston*	H6349	0 263 19143 5
Claiming His Family *Barbara Hannay*	H6350	0 263 19144 3
Wife and Mother Wanted *Nicola Marsh*	H6351	0 263 19145 1
The Tycoon's Double Trouble *Susan Meier*	H6352	0 263 19146 X
Instant Marriage, Just Add Groom *Myrna Mackenzie*		
	H6353	0 263 19147 8
The Consultant's Adopted Son *Jennifer Taylor*		
	H6354	0 263 19148 6
Mission: Mountain Rescue *Amy Andrews*	H6355	0 263 19149 4

HISTORICAL ROMANCE™

A Practical Mistress *Mary Brendan*	H627	0 263 19036 6
The Missing Heir *Gail Ranstrom*	H628	0 263 19037 4
The Gladiator's Honour *Michelle Styles*	H629	0 263 19038 2

MEDICAL ROMANCE™

| His Honourable Surgeon *Kate Hardy* | M537 | 0 263 19082 X |
| Pregnant with His Child *Lilian Darcy* | M538 | 0 263 19083 8 |

0206 Gen Std HB

MILLS & BOON®

Live the emotion

MARCH 2006 LARGE PRINT TITLES

ROMANCE™

The Disobedient Virgin *Sandra Marton*	1847	0 263 18939 2
A Scandalous Marriage *Miranda Lee*	1848	0 263 18940 6
Sleeping with a Stranger *Anne Mather*	1849	0 263 18941 4
At the Italian's Command *Cathy Williams*	1850	0 263 18942 2
Wife and Mother Forever *Lucy Gordon*	1851	0 263 18943 0
Christmas Gift: A Family *Barbara Hannay*	1852	0 263 18944 9
Mistletoe Marriage *Jessica Hart*	1853	0 263 18945 7
Taking on the Boss *Darcy Maguire*	1854	0 263 18946 5

HISTORICAL ROMANCE™

A Reputable Rake *Diane Gaston*	325	0 263 18903 1
Conquest Bride *Meriel Fuller*	326	0 263 18904 X
Princess of Fortune *Miranda Jarrett*	327	0 263 19068 4

MEDICAL ROMANCE™

The Italian Surgeon *Meredith Webber*	597	0 263 18859 0
A Nurse's Search and Rescue *Alison Roberts*	598	0 263 18860 4
The Doctor's Secret Son *Laura MacDonald*	599	0 263 18861 2
The Forever Assignment *Jennifer Taylor*	600	0 263 18862 0

0206 Gen Std LP

MILLS & BOON®

Live the emotion

APRIL 2006 HARDBACK TITLES

ROMANCE™

Prince of the Desert *Penny Jordan*	H6356	0 263 19150 8
For Pleasure...Or Marriage? *Julia James*	H6357	0 263 19151 6
The Italian's Price *Diana Hamilton*	H6358	0 263 19152 4
The Jet-Set Seduction *Sandra Field*	H6359	0 263 19153 2
His Private Mistress *Chantelle Shaw*	H6360	0 263 19154 0
Bertoluzzi's Heiress Bride *Catherine Spencer*		
	H6361	0 263 19155 9
Captive in His Bed *Sandra Marton*	H6362	0 263 19156 7
Kept by the Tycoon *Lee Wilkinson*	H6363	0 263 19157 5
Her Outback Protector *Margaret Way*	H6364	0 263 19158 3
The Sheikh's Secret *Barbara McMahon*	H6365	0 263 19159 1
A Woman Worth Loving *Jackie Braun*	H6366	0 263 19160 5
Her Ready-Made Family *Jessica Hart*	H6367	0 263 19161 3
The Nanny Solution *Susan Meier*	H6368	0 263 19162 1
A Taste of Paradise *Patricia Thayer*	H6369	0 263 19163 X
Maternal Instinct *Caroline Anderson*	H6370	0 263 19164 8
The Doctor's Proposal *Marion Lennox*	H6371	0 263 19165 6

HISTORICAL ROMANCE™

The Rogue's Kiss *Emily Bascom*	H630	0 263 19039 0
A Treacherous Proposition *Patricia Frances Rowell*		
	H631	0 263 19040 4
Rowan's Revenge *June Francis*	H632	0 263 19041 2

MEDICAL ROMANCE™

The Doctor's Marriage Wish *Meredith Webber*		
	M539	0 263 19084 6
The Surgeon's Perfect Match *Alison Roberts*		
	M540	0 263 19085 4

0306 Gen Std HB

MILLS & BOON®

Live the emotion

APRIL 2006 LARGE PRINT TITLES

ROMANCE™

Blackmailing the Society Bride *Penny Jordan*		
	1855	0 263 18958 9
Baby of Shame *Julia James*	1856	0 263 18959 7
Taken by the Highest Bidder *Jane Porter*	1857	0 263 18960 0
Virgin for Sale *Susan Stephens*	1858	0 263 18961 9
A Most Suitable Wife *Jessica Steele*	1859	0 263 18962 7
In the Arms of the Sheikh *Sophie Weston*		
	1860	0 263 18963 5
The Marriage Miracle *Liz Fielding*	1861	0 263 18964 3
Ordinary Girl, Society Groom *Natasha Oakley*		
	1862	0 263 18965 1

HISTORICAL ROMANCE™

The Outrageous Debutante *Anne O'Brien*	328	0 263 18905 8
The Captain's Lady *Margaret McPhee*	329	0 263 18906 6
Winter Woman *Jenna Kernan*	330	0 263 19069 2

MEDICAL ROMANCE™

Bride by Accident *Marion Lennox*	601	0 263 18863 9
Coming Home to Katoomba *Lucy Clark*	602	0 263 18864 7
The Consultant's Special Rescue *Joanna Neil*		
	603	0 263 18865 5
The Heroic Surgeon *Olivia Gates*	604	0 263 18866 3

0306 Gen Std LP